For Lily & Ale...

Hope my work makes you

BREATHLESS

erotica

KITTY TSUI

Kitty

Astraea Gala 1996

xx

**Firebrand
Books**

Kitty Tsui is also the author of *The Words of a Woman Who Breathes Fire*.

Several of these stories have appeared in earlier versions in *The Femme Mystique*, *Heat Wave*, *Intricate Passions*, *Pearls of Passion*, and *Queer View Mirror*.

Book and cover design by Nightwood Design
Front cover photograph by Jill Posener

Printed in the United States on acid-free paper by McNaughton & Gunn

10 9 8 7 6 5 4 3 2 1

Library of Congress Cataloging-in-Publication Data

Tsui, Kitty.
  Breathless : erotica / Kitty Tsui
      p.   cm.
  ISBN 1-56341-073-7 (cloth : alk. paper). —ISBN 1-56341-072-9 (paper : alk. paper)
    1. Lesbians—Sexual behavior—Fiction. 2. Erotic stories.
PS3570.S83674   1996
813'.54—dc20   95-1689
                                                            CIP

ACKNOWLEDGMENTS

There are many women I must thank.

My editor and publisher, Nancy K. Bereano
My agent, Sheryl Fullerton

My therapists, Roxanne and Margie
My chiropractors, Susan and Ann of Network Chiropractic

My girl dog, Meggie

Friends old and new: Kanani, my "twin"—Corinne, Zee, Doreena and Jenny, Trinity and Desirée, Jill and Lonna, Drusilla, Jan Dee, Lauren, Diana Lin, Ade, Luz, Linda, Lisa, Lisa K., Karen and Naria, Sarah, L.B., Lillian, Rhonda, Robin, Jo and Michele, Mikki, Mi Ok, Chrystos, Jill, Annie, Eleanor, Dorothy, Wendell, and Willyce

Anita Oñang for thirteen years of friendship

Thanks to k. and n., l., and x for their contribution to three stories

And the women who have peopled my life and my imagination, the women who touched me, held me, and loved me, the women who made me breathless.

All of them.

for Andrea,

friend, lover, soulmate

CONTENTS

breathless

i was born
a tough girl.
survived a childhood
of abuse and
abandonment.
found myself
through struggle
and years of
free-falling
through pain.

i am
a tough girl.
wear dark,
dark glasses
to hide
the emotions
in my eyes.
build my muscles
to shield myself
from pain,
from feelings.

i am
a tough girl.
not many things
make me gasp
for air.
to tell you
the truth
your kisses
make me
breathless.

vanilla and strawberries

One of the biggest advantages of working in the financial district is watching women on their lunch breaks. There are hundreds of them: hurrying to mail letters; buying yogurt, salad, or sandwiches; going to Nordstrom's or to the bank. There are women in skirts, stockings, and running shoes. Women in business suits and high heels. They wear hats, have their hair fashionably coifed, or loose and flying free. Some wear full makeup, others are totally without. Whatever their style, they all bring a smile to my face and help break up the monotony of a nine-to-five job.

I was sitting on a bench in the sun eating a hotdog when I saw her. The thing that struck me first was her salt-and-pepper hair. Actually, it was gray, but salt and pepper is probably the more de rigueur term. She had gray hair; it matched her charcoal pin-striped suit. She wore black-seamed stockings and black pumps, and carried a burgundy briefcase. She was a very striking woman at first glance. But then, I must confess, I do love older women, especially those who wear skirts.

She stood looking at her watch while waiting for the light to change. When her hand fell back to her side, I noticed the fingers drumming rapidly against her thigh.

I continued chewing on my hotdog, embellished with relish and extra onions, hoping the traffic light would not change. Being a shy girl I had no idea how to delay this woman for even a second. I did, however, regret the onions on my hotdog, even at this distance.

The light turned green. The woman with the striking gray hair hurried across the street and disappeared from my vision. I finished my hotdog and returned to my job.

I work in the graphics department of a large advertising agency. One of our most successful executives had just taken a leave. She'd found out that her recent weight gain was not the result of being wined and dined on a regular basis by grateful clients. According to her obstetrician, she was pregnant. Pearce and Pearce Advertising Associates was seeking someone to fill her position.

It was a Friday and a record-breaking hot day. The receptionist had called in sick, something I wished I had been able to do. And although I had a pile of my own work, being the newly hired staff person, I was assigned to sit at the front desk.

Somewhat resentful at having to answer phones and smile at prospective clients while neglecting my own deadlines, I brightened when the gray-haired woman walked through the door.

"I have an appointment," she announced briskly, "with Brandon Pearce."

"Uh...yes," I replied, stammering like an adolescent, "your name, please."

"Jayne," she answered, "with a *y.* Smyth, also with a *y.*"

"Have a seat," I said, playing the receptionist role to the hilt. "I'll let him know you're here."

The receptionist returned to work on Monday, a typically foggy San Francisco summer day. Jayne Smyth joined Pearce and Pearce Advertising Associates the following week.

I have certain rules I try to adhere to that govern my behavior as a nice Chinese girl. One, I do not get involved with anyone on the job. Two, I am not interested in straight women. And three, women who do not like my dog do not stay long in my bed.

Jayne Smyth is originally from Great Britain, as am I, though she comes from London while I was born in Hong Kong. She is ten years older than I. We hit it off immediately, discovering that we had similarities in our backgrounds and experiences.

I found her very attractive, whether in dresses, tailored suits or designer ensembles. When I told her I was a lesbian, she replied that we had something else in common. I was thrilled.

Rules and regulations are the cornerstones of society. Three thousand years of Chinese civilization had certainly taught me that. Being a contemporary woman, however, and a feminist to boot, I was convinced that some rules were meant to be broken. Early in our acquaintance I learned that Jayne loved dogs. Since she was not straight, the only other hurdle was the fact that we worked together.

I'm good at rationalizations, and I rationalized it quite simply: I was a graphic designer and she was an account executive. So what if we were employed by the same company? We were in totally separate departments.

We frequently lunched together. We never talked about work. The sexual tension between us grew so unbearable that we began to find excuses not to eat together.

"Can't today. I'm on deadline."

"I've got a lunch meeting."

"Gotta run to the bank. Maybe next week."

When we bumped into each other in the coffee room or at the copy machine, we avoided each other's eyes.

Finally I could stand it no longer. I called her from my desk.

"Hi."

"Hullo."

"Listen—"

"Yes?"

"Well, I...look—"

"What's up? I really can't talk now. I've got to take a conference call in five minutes."

"Okay, I'll be quick. It's been almost a month since you started working at the agency and lunching together's been the extent of our activities," I began. "How about dinner at my place tonight?" It was the Friday before the Fourth of July, the start of a long holiday weekend. I figured she already had plans.

Jayne sighed at the other end of the line, a few offices away.

"Okay, sure. Sounds great. What shall I bring?"

Jayne came over at seven. We started with seltzer, salt-free tortilla chips, guacamole, and salsa. Meggie loved her because Jayne fed her tortilla chips minus the salsa. We listened to Billie Holiday and K.T. Oslin. I fixed poached salmon, wilted spinach salad with bacon and crushed peppercorns, and sourdough baguettes. After dinner we contemplated going to the movies but couldn't decide on one. We sat on the couch and petted the dog. This continued for what seemed like an awfully long time.

All kinds of questions went through my mind: Want to look at my portfolio? Like show tunes? Do you line dance? Should we go for a walk with the dog? What I really wanted to say was, "Wanna fuck?" But seeing that she was from another generation, I thought it might not be the appropriate thing.

Instead I said, "I have ice cream in the fridge. Strawberries, too, if you're not into sugar."

"What kind of ice cream do you have?" she asked. "I'm very particular about my ice cream."

"Me, too," I replied. "I only like one kind of ice cream."

"What kind's that?

"Vanilla bean."

"Hmm, vanilla and strawberries. Great combination. Ever eaten in the tub?"

"Uh, excuse me?" I said, in a bit of a shock.

"Haven't you ever had ice cream and strawberries in the bathtub?"

"Well, as a matter of fact, no."

"Want to give it a try?"

"Uh, well," I stumbled, trying to keep my composure.

"You know what Tina Turner said, don't you?"

"What's that?"

"I'll try *anything* one time."

"I'm not sure I'm as daring as Tina Turner. Well, what can I say?"

"Say you're game," she teased, looking me straight in the eye.

"All right, Jayne. I'm game."

Jayne dished the ice cream into big bowls and washed the long-stemmed strawberries. I filled the tub, lit some candles, and put my yellow rubber ducks into the water.

Jayne came into the bathroom and undressed me. She kissed my neck and bit my bare shoulders. She unbuttoned my jeans and pulled them off, one leg at a time. She slipped off my socks and kissed the tops of my feet.

"Get into the water," she smiled. "I'll feed you."

I did as I was told, finding it not altogether unpleasant to take orders from her. Jayne fed me strawberries and ice cream while I luxuriated in the water. I took the sweet berries in my mouth and licked ice cream from her fingers. Warmth enveloped me up to my neck. Heat rose from between my legs.

Jayne washed me with the lavender soap. She

scrubbed my back and ass with a loofah, took my toes into her mouth and sucked on them. I moaned and squeezed my rubber ducks. She put her hand between my thighs and opened me up to her fingers. I felt the rush of water entering my inner lips as she pushed inside me.

"Aren't you glad you listened to Tina?" she laughed.

The candles were burning low as I got out of the tub. Jayne took a towel and patted my body dry. She got down on her knees between my legs and took me in her mouth.

I'm so glad I listened to Tina Turner. *Private dancer, better be good to me.*

flesh to flesh

The flame of the candle threw a yellow light on her skin. The end of the cigarette glowed as she inhaled. She blew the smoke out and turned her face to me.

"I love the way you make me feel."

"Ditto," I smiled, as I drew circles on her flat belly.

"I think I..."

"Careful," I interrupted. "You're thinking too much. And don't say anything you may regret. We just met, remember?"

"I was only going to say that—"

"No more words, okay. Put out your cigarette and roll over for me."

"Now?"

"No, next week. What do you think?"

She complied without another word.

I ran my hand from her neck down her spine to the crack between her cheeks. She shivered and her buttocks quivered.

"Hold still."

"But I—"

"And don't say another word."

I moved to lie on top of her, my breasts pressed to her back, groin to ass, thigh to thigh, flesh to flesh. I licked at the soft fuzz on the nape of her neck. Breathed in the scent of her hair. Took her ear in my mouth and explored the crevices with my tongue. Her whole body responded in a throaty moan.

"You weren't supposed to speak," I growled, grabbing a mouthful of flesh and biting hard.

"Owwww," she screamed.

"What did I say?" I bore down harder with my teeth.

Her body shook in silent sobs, but no sounds came out of her mouth.

I released my hold on her shoulder.

"That's better. It's always better when you do as you're told."

I licked the tender spot, caressing the indentations made by my teeth. Trailed my fingers across her shoulders.

"There. Does that feel better?"

Silence.

"Amy, you okay? Don't play dumb with me. I know you like to be bitten, and the harder the better."

She turned her head to look at me, a wounded look in her eyes.

"What?"

Still she would not speak.

"Okay, come on. Talk to me now."

"That hurt," she whispered.

"But was it a good hurt or a bad hurt?"

"It just hurt," she snapped. "I didn't like it."

"Why didn't you use your safe word then? That's what it's for."

"I didn't want to."

"Why not? I don't know how much you can take. You have to tell me. That's what safe words are for, so that you can direct me. I am a sadist but I'm not one of those brutal tops. Especially not with a novice. Pain is not supposed to be unpleasant. I can push you to your limits, but you've got to be the one to set them."

She had tears in her eyes.

"Come here and lie in my arms. Just let me hold you for a while."

I held her close to me, wiped the tears from her face.

After a time she began to touch my breasts. She took my nipple in her mouth and sucked like a hungry baby. I stroked her hair. Suddenly she broke away from me, sparks flying from her eyes.

"Turn over," she ordered.

I did so.

She lay pressed on top of me, flesh to flesh. Her teeth moved down my back, teasing, biting, grabbing at skin. When she reached my buttocks, her tongue began to lick my cheeks. I moaned contentedly.

"Quiet," she snapped, "or I'll stop. Do you hear me?"

I nodded.

"Good," she replied, "it's always better when you do as you're told."

But she did stop. I felt her getting off the bed, heard a drawer open and close. Then she lay on top of my legs, pinning me to the bed with her weight. Her face close to my ass. All of a sudden I felt a finger coated with cold lube probing at my asshole. She spread the lube all over, stretched a dental dam over my crack, and drew her tongue along the crack, round and round my hole.

It took a great effort for me to keep quiet. Mighty roars gathered on my lips, on the verge of bursting. There is no feeling in the world that can compare to being rimmed.

Amy was relentless with her mouth and her tongue. I squirmed and ground my hips into the bed. But I held my silence.

"You're being so good," she said. "I know how my tongue in your ass affects you. You just want to scream. Now I'm going to give you something else you love. And you're going to hold your tongue and just take it quietly. Right?"

I raised my head and nodded, grinning like a fool.

"Good. Like you said, 'It's always better when you do as you're told.'"

"Hi. It's past midnight here so it must be after three your time. Did I wake you?"

"Umm, yes, but I was just dozing. Can't really sleep, it's so hot and humid here. Thunderstormed earlier." Carley yawned and pulled the sheets from between her damp thighs. "I think I was dreaming about you."

"Oh? What? A good dream I hope."

"Don't really remember, but I imagine it was good. You always are. You were just here. When the phone rang it startled me. You're the only one who calls me this late. And I thought you were in bed with me."

"Wish I were. Sorry I woke you."

"It's okay. You know I like it when you wake me."

"I have insomnia again. Don't know what's wrong with me, but I hate it when I can't sleep. It would be great if I could come over and crawl into bed with you."

"Come on, then! How fast can you drive from San Francisco to New York?" Carley laughed.

"If I borrow Mariko's Beamer and break some speed records, maybe ten minutes. Can you wait that long?"

"Uh-huh. Fifteen minutes max, though. I'll even have coffee and cake waiting for you when you get here."

"Coffee and cake won't be the only things I'll want, darling."

"That hungry, are you? Shall I fix a four-course meal or will bacon and eggs do?"

"I'm hungry for you. Move over and let me get into bed with you. You are alone, aren't you?"

"I never sleep alone, dear, you should know that. There's a gray furball in bed next to me."

"Well, move that fat cat 'cause I'm on my way. I'll have to get ready in a hurry if I'm going to be there in fifteen minutes. Don't have time to dress in full leather. What would you like to see me in?"

"Your black teddy will do just fine."

"Don't want to cause any accidents on the road. You know Mariko's car doesn't have tinted windows."

"Honey, it's dark and you'll be driving very fast. Who's going to see you? Okay, if you insist. Hmm, let me see. How about wearing your jeans and denim jacket over the teddy. They're easy to take off. Oh, and make sure you're in your 501s."

"Certainly. Anything to oblige a lady. I'll even bring along my black leather gloves, safe sex supplies, and a big tube of lube. Are you awake now?"

Carley laughed her deep, throaty laugh. "What do you think?"

"I think you're wide awake and already wet."

"Oh, baby, I think you're right."

"Why don't you touch yourself and tell me how wet you are."

"I'm very wet. Come over, please. I can't wait fifteen minutes."

"You'll have to wait. You'll have to wait as long as I tell you to wait. What are you wearing?"

"Nothing. I just have black panties on."

"Take them off for me. Slowly. Hand them to me so I can smell you. Umm. You smell great. You smell as good as I know you taste. What color sheets are on your bed?"

"They're the color of Devon cream. With lace around the edges. I just bought them. Tonight's the first night I'm sleeping on them."

"Really? Great. You know I love the feel of new

sheets. Turn over on your stomach so I can see your ass. Put your arms up above your head and open your legs as wide as they'll go. I want to see you all stretched out on your new creamy sheets. My hands are on your body, stroking the length of your neck, tracing the muscles along your back, kneading the curves of your thighs. I'm kissing the dimples in your ass."

Mel paused. She could hear Carley's cries.

"Oh, Mel, oh, baby, I'm so hot for you. Give it to me, please. Oh, honey, please. Oh, baby, I want it all. I want as much as you can give me."

"I'm turned on too. I can feel my wetness through the denim."

"Baby, please fuck me. Please."

"Not yet. You know you like it when I make you wait. Isn't that right?"

"Yes, baby, yes...oh, but I can't wait."

"Yes, yes, you can. Yes you can, baby. I'm taking your ass in my mouth and biting you hard, running my tongue down your crack, licking your cheeks. I'm so turned on I can hardly wait to push inside you. I want to feel the whole force of my body inside you. Turn over and let me kiss you. Take my tongue inside you and suck on it. Oh yes, yes. Your breasts are so full in my hands, your nipples so hard. I'm taking them in my mouth. I'm biting you."

"Oh, God, Mel, I want to come."

"No, Carley. No. Not till I say so. I'm going to take you in my mouth, wrap my lips round your clitoris. Can you feel me sucking you?"

"Ahh, aaahhh."

"My hands are on your nipples, my tongue licking your folds. Your juices are all over my mouth. You smell so good. I can't stop sucking on your clit. You taste so good and I want you so bad."

"Baby, I'm dripping wet for you."

"Good, baby. I'm really turned on, too. Can you feel my wetness through my jeans? Kiss me, Carley. Kiss me until I feel the distance between us closing, until I'm in your bed and your legs are wrapped around me."

"Yes, Mel, yes. I can feel you here. I can feel your hands and smell your heat."

"Do you want me, baby?"

"Honey, you know I do. I want all of you. I want as much as you can give. I want you to push me really far. I want you to take me hard. I want to not think for a while, just feel. Please take me, honey. Fuck me, please."

"You're so hot and wet. My fingers are circling your clitoris, stroking your folds. I want to enter you with all of my being. I want you to feel the power of my body as I love you. Can you take it?"

"Honey," Carley moaned. "Please, yes...yes. I want to touch your body, your strong thighs in your tight jeans. I want to feel the muscles in your ass. I want your strong arms around me. I'm so hot for you, honey. Take me, please, take me."

"You're dripping wet for me, baby. I want to push inside you with all the power in me. I want to penetrate you with my fingers. Can you feel me inside you? Two fingers. Three, four. I want to slide my thumb inside your wetness. Relax, baby, open up to me. Let me rub your clitoris hard and fast. Feel my fingers enter you, curl and lodge inside your cunt in the place where fire is raging. My knuckles are straining to enter you. You know when I get excited I can't wait to push inside you. My mouth is on your mouth, my fingers squeezing your nipple, my fist lodged deep in your cunt. Do you feel me moving inside you?"

"Oh, baby, don't stop. Please don't stop, baby."

"Give it to me, Carley, come for me. Give me everything you've got."

Mel could feel her power, the motion, her fist lodged inside her lover. She could feel Carley's heat enveloping her whole hand and hear her cries of pleasure. Carley came to orgasm in great spasms that gripped and rocked Mel's fist.

"I love you, baby," they echoed, in unison.

"Come lie in my arms," Mel whispered. "Come lie in my arms and let me hold you."

The fragrance of night-blooming jasmine drifted in through the open window. Mel could feel Carley's heartbeat on her breast as surely as she could feel the damp wetness in the crotch of her 501s.

When Mel woke up the next morning, her cordless phone lay on top of the tangled sheets along with her jeans.

one-night stand

Clean sheets. Lee lay naked in the big bed luxuriating in the feel of them. Clean sheets with their particular feel and smell. Clean sheets were one of her favorite things. That and a walk by the sea. Bare feet on warm sand. Ice-cold sparkling apple cider. Chinese roast duck over white rice. Her beloved ten-year-old vizsla. Anything made of black leather. Kissing soft lips.

It was a Saturday. A day spent doing the usual chores, not altogether unpleasant. She had a leisurely morning drinking lattes and reading through an accumulation of the week's newspapers. Then she took her dog to the beach. The afternoon was reserved for grocery shopping and doing the laundry. Lee loved planning meals, and clean clothes.

After the chores it was still early. Lee lay on the fresh-smelling sheets and surveyed her home with satisfaction. Things were clean and dust-free. The laundry had been put away. Books were in their place. Even the towels in the bathroom had been folded just so. She smiled and leaned over to pet her dog, stretched out asleep beside her. Lee liked it when everything was in its place. Orderliness gave her a sense of control.

Lee closed her eyes and started touching herself. When her nipples began to respond, she took them between her thumb and index finger and gave them a sustained pinch. She could feel the juices welling up hot between her legs. She turned onto her stomach, positioning her cunt on top of her hands. Slowly, her pelvis started to move. Slowly at first, then faster and faster, her bare ass moved in a patch of afternoon sun. Soon the silence was broken by her short, sharp cries.

Lee was dozing when M.J. came into her mind. Lee had met her in New York some years ago while on a business trip. On her last night in Manhattan she had gone to the Duchess, a lesbian bar. She had planned to have a quick Perrier before returning to her hotel. But that was before she saw M.J.

M.J. had been standing at the bar smoking a cigarette and listening with feigned interest to a discussion about separatist politics. She was smiling a crooked smile, as if she knew a secret that was hers alone.

She was a round woman who seemed defiant and proud of her body. And she was light enough to pass, if her nose and her lips didn't give her away. She followed Lee with her eyes from the moment Lee walked by her at the bar. Lee hadn't finished half her drink when the woman approached her and said, "Hi, I'm M.J. and I've never seen you here before."

Lee liked her directness.

M.J. said, "Don't see too many Asian women here. I love Asian women. I'm one too, you know. Well, I should say I'm Asian American. And I'm a half and half."

"Oh," Lee replied, "me too. Asian American, I mean. Oh, that's silly," she laughed, "as if you couldn't tell. You know, I hate it when I go to a bookstore and ask for Asian American literature. I'm directed to Kabuki, kite-making, or Oriental Studies. Once I was taken to the Chinese cookbooks. Asian American literature? I don't get it."

"Yeah, I did that at the local library and they asked me if I wanted the books in English. Of course I want them in English! We're here, don't they know that? We're Americans too." She frowned as she talked, but her voice was light. "My real name's May Jade. When I was a kid my mother played mah-jongg all the time and she'd use M.J. for short. So it stuck. Everyone calls me M.J. And can't you just see a Black Chinese dyke answering to the name May Jade White?"

They laughed together and talked easily. Both related to growing up in a Chinese household with grandparents they called *poa poa* and *gung gung*. Both admitted to liking Asian women, and later on, to liking each other. They talked and danced until the bar closed. Lee wanted to ask M.J. to spend the night with her, but instead said, "Want to go for noodles in Chinatown?"

It was five on a chilly spring morning when they hailed a cab on Canal Street to take them uptown. Inside, in the warmth, Lee took M.J.'s face in her hands and kissed her full on the lips. She could not draw herself away. M.J.'s lips were soft and warm, surely the softest lips she'd ever kissed.

The cabbie drove through the night. City lights, traffic sped by. M.J. flirted with Lee, throwing looks from piercing gray eyes. Tickled her earlobes with quick darts of her tongue. Kissed her relentlessly, hard on the lips, her tongue insistent.

Suddenly Lee pulled away and said breathlessly, "But you're with someone."

"You're not," came the reply.

"We're in a taxi, a moving vehicle." Lee tried again.

"You think we're the first ones in his cab to be doing this?" M.J. laughed. "Your next excuse will be that you're a nice Chinese girl."

"I am...you are...we were—"

But M.J. was unbuttoning Lee's shirt and kissing her skin.

"I want you," she whispered. "I want you real bad."

Lee looked up and saw the bright eyes of the cabbie watching them in the rearview mirror.

"I don't think we should be doing this. The guy's looking at us—"

"Oh, baby, hush. Oh, your skin is so smooth. I could just lick you all over."

"Come up to my hotel room with me and I'll let you."

"Umm, baby, I can't. Let me start on you here. Let me just do you right now."

Lee pulled away from her with some difficulty. "Are you nuts? Do you have a thing about public sex or something? I don't want you to think I'm some kind of uptight prude, but really."

M.J. just laughed and continued to lick her neck.

The next thing Lee knew, the taxi had stopped at the hotel. She couldn't believe it when M.J. had insisted on going home.

"I'm expected," was all she said. "I'm already past being late. Call me if you're ever out this way again." And she was gone.

Lee watched the taillights until the cab turned the corner and was out of sight. She was angry and restless and couldn't sleep. She spent the next few hours pacing in her hotel room until it was time to go to the airport. She was upset that M.J.'s flirtation had been just a tease. She was upset that her body had responded, that M.J. had fired her up from the wetness between her legs to the tingling in her toes.

Lee hated having insomnia, even if it was already dawn. And she hated being rejected on her last night in New York City. Couldn't even call it a one-night stand.

The telephone rang, jolting her from her reverie.

"Is this Lee?" asked a voice she couldn't quite place.

"Yes, speaking."

"This is M.J." There was a long pause. "I hope you remember me."

Lee drew in her breath sharply. You've done it again, she thought to herself. You've conjured her up and now she's here.

"I'm on my way to L.A. and have a free night. I'm really sorry about the way things were left the last time. It's complicated being monogamous sometimes. I'm single now," she blurted. Then the voice hesitated. "I'd like to see you tonight. Is that possible?"

One part of Lee thought, Great. There's food in the fridge and the house is clean. I'm free tonight and I'd love to see her. But the demon shouted, Fuck her. She teased you, rejected you, and dumped you. Forget it.

"I'd like to see you, too, but I have to tell you last time was difficult. I was hurt because I felt like you teased me and then left with some excuse about your lover."

"I wanted to sleep with you, but it would have been just too complicated. That's why I left."

Lee sighed and said, "Come on over."

M.J. was dressed in tight black pants and a white silk shirt. Red Reeboks shone on her feet. Lee had been somewhat tense, not knowing what to expect from the meeting. But when she opened the door and saw M.J. she burst out, with a loud laugh, "You look more like a Californian than a New Yorker. Look at you!"

She could not hide the pleasure in her voice.

"Surprise, girl. I am a Californian. I've been living in New York on a scholarship. I may be moving back to the West Coast."

Lee drew her close and kissed her without any hesitation. Many minutes passed before Lee realized that they were standing in the doorway and the front door was wide open.

"Come in," she said. "Want some tea? You hungry or anything?"

"I'm hungry, oh, yes I am," M.J. replied, her voice

a low growl. "I've been thinking about you since the day we rode around Manhattan in the back of the cab. I'd like to eat you. I'd like to have you right now."

Lee took off M.J.'s red shoes, her pants, shirt, and white lace underwear. She kissed M.J. all over until she thought she would faint with desire. Lee pinned M.J. under her body, and, starting at the core, stroked her clitoris, her nipples, her neck, her mouth.

M.J. held onto Lee's solid, muscular body and opened herself up to her mouth and her hands. She was wet when Lee's fingers found her opening, and she shuddered when Lee plunged inside her with a power she had never felt before. They moved together in a rhythm that was strong, deep, and steady.

M.J. came to orgasm in a way that was new for her. Lee's hand was inside her, Lee's mouth on her clitoris. All of M.J.'s awareness was centered on her cunt. Lee's fist pounded inside her in a delicious rhythm that was at first painful, but was now generating incredible waves of pleasure. She felt herself tense, peak with pleasure, open and open, shuddering uncontrollably in the release. M.J. expected Lee to stop when she felt her orgasm, so she gasped and cried out when it was apparent that Lee was not finished.

"Keep coming for me, baby. Yes, that's right, yes, yes," Lee hissed as she moved and thrust and brought M.J. to orgasm after orgasm with each stroke. "Yeah, baby, I know you've been waiting for this. Let me fuck you and fill you and make you feel so good."

It was way past midnight when passion released them. Lee put on an oversized shirt and went into the kitchen.

"Still hungry?" she grinned. "We've got lots of choices here tonight. If you're too hungry to wait we can have tea and toast, or a bowl of Top Ramen. On second thought," she continued, without giving the other woman a chance to get a word in, "how about an omelet. And maybe some fried rice?"

"Darlin', I'll eat anything with you right now," M.J. smiled. "Anything."

Lee went back to the bed and ran her hand along the length of M.J.'s body.

"If I fix you a great meal, will you come again?"

"Uh-huh. You bet I will, baby."

"You're a beautiful woman," Lee said with great tenderness. "And I love those lips of yours."

She bent to kiss her, gathering her up in her arms.

"Oh, baby," M.J. moaned. "How about I come again before your great meal? Umm. You're so good. Besides, I never did like them one-night stands."

a femme in butch clothing

I am fascinated by body parts. There's tits and ass. And ass and legs. Ass and thighs. Thighs excite me. Hard, muscular thighs. Thunder thighs. Kind, open thighs. Also rounded biceps and long forearms. And then there are lips. Full lips. Soft lips. Lips painted some shade of red. Or unpainted but flushed with blood from a long session of rough kissing. Lips moving down my inner thigh then up the length of my quadricep. Lips wrapped around the dildo anchored in the crotch of my 501s. Teeth bearing down on my bicep. Teeth teasing my skin. Teeth sinking into my flesh.

Body parts. There's back and shoulders. Big back. Broad shoulders. Breasts that fill my hands. Dark brown nipples. Firm forearms. Unyielding knees that hold her legs open. There's the convex roundness of a stomach. The line of her neck. The curve of a cheekbone. The hint of a smile. The bulge of a bicep. The horseshoe of a tricep. There are soft, sweet toes, delicate ankles and a gently contoured heel.

I've been a practicing lesbian for over two decades now, and women still fascinate me. The way a woman moves. Strides. Struts. That certain look in her eyes. Sure. Seductive. Or shy but begging to be taken. The way she flips her hair back off her face in an arrogant sort of way. Especially when she knows I'm watching her every move. And she knows I love watching her every move.

Let me tell you about my femme. She has long black hair and stands five foot seven in her stockinged feet. That's tall for a Chinese woman. Her nails are short but perfectly manicured. Sometimes she paints them a shade of red called Real Ruby, but only when we're going into the bedroom, not out on the town. Her breasts are soft, sweet as ripe mangoes.

She wears plain white T-shirts, blue jeans, and Reeboks. And she has a black motorcycle jacket. A Schott. That's her uniform most of the time. When she's not at work, that is. She wears her hair long and loose. She likes to look at a man straight in the eye, toss her hair back in that certain way as if to say, *I'm beautiful. I'm a lesbian. And you can't have me.*

The first time I saw her she turned my head. I had attended a matinee performance of *Phantom of the Opera.* I was standing at a nearby street corner with a group of theater-goers, all dutifully obeying the light, when a woman dressed in leather strode confidently through the congested jigsaw of cars. Drivers stared. Some gaped. But no one honked their horn. She was dressed all in leather. Leather shirt. Leather pants. Leather boots. Black leather. Now this was the middle of summer in Chicago, not San Francisco! She looked cool—and very, very hot.

She caught my eye and gave me a look: *I know you know I'm one, just like you.* She deliberately walked close and smiled at me boldly. I caught a whiff of her perfume. It was Shalimar, my favorite.

In my opinion, there is nothing so erotically charged as a woman dressed in leather. I disentangled myself from the crowd and followed her like a puppy. Halfway down the street, she turned to me and said, "Walk beside me. I know you're no slave. Anyway, what I'm looking for is a butch top or a butch bottom. Or better yet, a butch switch, but not a slave."

Believe it or not, that's how we met.

It's hard to say exactly what my favorite body part

is. My tastes seem to vary from woman to woman. Time to time. But I do like ass. Hers in particular. But really any ass will do. Spare and hard and tight. Large and round and pliable. In denim or in lace. In leather or in a harness. In bikini bottoms or a jockstrap. In flannel Jockeys or silk boxers. White cotton Calvins or Victoria's Secret lace. She doesn't always bother with panties. She knows that when I get excited foreplay doesn't exist. I want to get to the core of things quickly.

I like to watch her ass. Sometimes when we're out walking, I'll lag a few steps behind so I can look at the muscles move in her ass. Oh, yes, I like her ass when it's up in the air. I like her ass when she's straddling my back. I like her ass when she's bent over my face.

Women fascinate me. The way they move. Moan. Smell. Smile. Sigh. The way they hold cigarettes. Hold my wrist. Cross their legs. Spread their legs. Lick their lips. Lick my cock.

My femme enjoys playing. She wears leather and lace dresses, a garter belt and black-seamed stockings. She knows I like them. Sometimes, on her way to the bedroom, she paints her face, and like a chameleon, transforms herself from femme to high-femme. Ordinarily she uses no makeup. She knows I like her best unadorned, just the way she is. She puts on her highest pair of stiletto heels and doesn't bother with panties.

I force her down on her hands and knees, play with the breasts that are hanging down in front of her. I tease her ass with my tongue, torment her thighs with my touch. I like to enter her slow so she can feel every inch. I hold her as I thrust into her and fuck her good and hard the way I know she wants it.

Sometimes I tie her down spread-eagle on the bed. With leather restraints lined with lamb's wool. Other times I tie her up with leather thongs that bite. I strap on my biggest dildo and parade in front of her, cradling its weight in my hand. Sometimes I lavish her body with kisses until she begs me to push inside her. Sometimes I'll thrust into her with no foreplay, knowing she's as wet as ocean spray. I'll thrust into her relentlessly, till she screams and sobs and cries out my name. And when she explodes, I refuse to let her stop.

I like it that she's Chinese. We have a common language and culture, even though she was born in the Midwest and I was born in the Far East. And I speak Cantonese and she doesn't. Her second language is French. I like it that I don't always have to explain, educate, or entertain. We share the same love for learning and leather. For food. Food is a very esoteric thing. And we Chinese enjoy an esoteric farrago of food.

To name a few, there's *jook* for breakfast, *dim sum* for lunch, and tofu with liquid cane sugar for dessert. Fermented black beans. Fermented bean curd. Squab. Squid. Conch. Oxtails. Oyster sauce. Fish sauce. Sea cucumber. Bitter melon. Winter melon. Peanut and chicken-feet soup. Steamed pork with ham yu, salty fish. Taro root and beef tendons. Sweet almond soup.

My femme is as skilled in the kitchen as she is in the bedroom. She can handle a blade as well as a fist. She can stir-fry as well as she can kiss, beat cream as well as she can unroll a condom.

We play in the kitchen as much as we do in the bedroom. The kitchen floor can attest to that. I've fucked her against the wall, too, but it's better for me if she's up on the countertop. The easier it is on my back, the more endurance I have for her. That ancient book, the *I Ching*, says it right: *Perseverance furthers.*

She fixes me chicken with shiitake mushrooms in her leather bustier. Steamed rock cod with ginger and scallions. Rock salt shrimp. Southern fried chicken with country gravy. Pot roast melting in juice. Fried noodles in the nude. Steamed rice. We eat rice with every meal.

White rice. She fixes me Earl Grey tea in the middle of the afternoon with homemade shortbread. Hot tea in a glass tumbler. Very Chinese.

She feeds me with her fingers. I suck the length of them the way I suck the flesh out of a crab claw. She eats ice cream off my chest, licks me in the places where it dribbles. She drinks from my mouth.

She is my femme in butch clothing. She wears 501s, leather chaps, work boots, and men's shirts on the street. Cashmere, silk, or satin to bed. She knows the fastest way to undo my pants and the fastest way to bring me to multiple orgasms with her mouth on my clitoris.

She told me the first thing she noticed about me was that I was Chinese. The second was the size of my hands. I am the first. I told her it would hurt, but she was game. I take her without hesitation. Hard and driving. Deep and slow. In full control. I stroke the core of her pleasure over and over. And I refuse to let her go.

those lips

Practically the first thing she said to me was: "Those lips! Those lips of yours were made to be kissed. Full and moist, those lips were made to be parted and penetrated by eager tongues."

It was in this way that she began her flirtation with me.

For once, I was single and very available. Unfortunately, she was a married woman. Though that had never stopped me before, and didn't now.

We met often for mochas at Café Flore on Market Street and popcorn in dark movie houses in the middle of the day. She whispered dirty secrets to me, tickling my earlobe with her breath and her tongue.

One night she told the girlfriend she was going back to the office and met me in the Mission. After a meal of burritos, she kissed me, the taste of cilantro and chili peppers still on her tongue.

"Not here," I said. "Besides, you're married."

She laughed.

"You should be more worried about teenage boys than my girlfriend!"

She leaned in for another kiss. I tried to conjure up images of the girlfriend, hoping this would halt the heat spreading between my legs, but she kissed me until I gasped for breath and all images of the girlfriend had melted into the night air.

"I want you," she said. "I want to feel your body moving under mine. I want to spread your lips wide and push inside you. I want to hear you moan and call out my name. I want to make you come twice for all the nights you've ever spent alone in your bed."

She deceived her girlfriend for almost a year. One night she left the house, telling the girlfriend she needed to be alone. We met for drinks in a bar and started making out, the way we always did. Then the girlfriend walked in. It was over for them.

In retrospect, it started almost from the moment we began living together. Lesbian bed death set in quicker than you could say "JoAnn Loulan." I was the happy femme homemaker, she the butch breadwinner. I raised the child—okay, the dog—kept house, shopped for groceries, and performed all the domestic management duties. To perfection, if I may say so myself. She worked a nine-to-five job.

When she got home from work she changed into grubbies, sat down to a homecooked meal, read the newspaper, and watched TV. On Saturday nights we ate dinner out, went to a movie, returned home to walk the dog, then retired to bed. And a book.

Some nights I would wear my black teddy to bed, the one with the snaps in the crotch.

"We'll do it this weekend," she'd say, turning away.

But come the weekend she'd have started bleeding and cramps were just around the corner. Or she was stressed out from her job. Or she was too tired. More often than not, she just plain forgot about our plans. Finally I gave up. The spontaneity was gone and our scheduled dates forgotten. I put the teddy and the silk pajamas away. What was the use of trying? She hugged her pillow. I spooned the dog.

We took each other for granted. I took for granted that she'd always bring home the bacon. She took for granted that I'd spend my life cooking and cleaning for her. She got moody, I became distant. Our silences grew.

The only things we said to each other were: "What's the weather going to be like tomorrow?" "Change the channel, would you?" "When are you going to pick up the dry cleaning?" "Want seconds?" "Don't forget my prescription at Walgreen's." And, "Rice again?" Yes, rice again, I wanted to reply. I'm Chinese. I can eat rice three times a day and would except for the fact that I live with a *lofan,* a white girl.

And, of course, we said: "I love you." "Me, too."

I got suspicious when she started meeting someone from the office for dinner every week. This is after she had previously been adamant about not fraternizing with her subordinates at work. When she and I went out to eat we'd dress in our grubbies and be gone for an hour, two at the most. But when she went out with Letticia, she'd dress up and be gone for five or six. One night they watched *Sleepless in Seattle* and *Prelude to a Kiss.* Uh-huh. We never did double features; she claimed she couldn't sit that long. They saw each other at work every day but they would talk every night. Business, she'd say. Uh-huh. Letticia sometimes called as late as eleven-thirty. Didn't she know we went to bed at ten? And there were many hang ups. Doesn't every girl get suspicious about hang ups?

One evening I was sitting in the living room painting my nails when she said we had to talk. Uh-huh? But she hemmed and hawed, then left abruptly to go to the office. She was beginning to put in some very long hours.

Just then the phone rang. When the machine answered, the caller hung up. 415-334-7551. Letticia. I had just bought a caller ID unit. I burst into tears. Though my mascara ran, crying made me feel much better. I went into the kitchen to make tea. While I waited for it to brew, I drew up a list:

Things I am not getting from the relationship:

1. Sex
2. Emotional support
3. Friendship
4. Intimacy
5. Affection
6. Sex

I also made a list of things I *was* getting from the relationship, but there was only one item on it. I tore up the piece of paper and threw it in the garbage.

So began our six-month process of divorcing. To say that it was difficult would be a gross understatement, but I will not bore you with the details. Just believe me when I tell you that it was hell.

I finally moved out with my dog and rented a studio apartment near Hayes Street Park. It's tough being single, especially if you're over twenty-five.

Recently I noticed that I have no interest in women. I don't even look at them anymore. Now that's a real shocker! I am a girl who has always loved to cruise butches. What happened? I'm not that old, am I? I thought a woman's sex drive was supposed to pick up when she hit forty.

I didn't know how much the relationship made me feel undesirable and unattractive until I was out of it. It was not a pretty picture. Thank goodness for my shrink and my dog.

I joined a gym and started working out with weights. Bought a new swimsuit and swam twice a week. I signed up with a temp agency and they're getting me some good gigs. Nothing to write home about, but hey, it's a start. And no one knows better than me that I need a new start.

Last night was Saturday. Date night. I soaked in a bubble bath. Then put on a new dress and fixed my face. I made myself stir-fried chicken and asparagus over rice. For a side dish I cut up cocktail tomatoes and marinated them in garlic, basil, and olive oil. I lit candles and set an elaborate table for myself. I enjoyed a leisurely meal, not allowing myself to read or watch TV while I ate.

After dinner I put on my teddy and climbed into bed with the latest issue of *Girlfriends*. Cecilia, the centerfold, tried to lure me to her bed. But she was wearing lacy black underwear, and I much prefer my girls in boxer shorts or jockstraps. In combat boots rather than stiletto heels. I'm the one who wears the heels in this house! Goodnight, Cecilia.

I lay on my back, eyes closed, and thought of Jen, my first love. She was more androgynous than butch but she was my first. The earth shook when we made love. And she knew how to kiss. She could make me come just by kissing me.

The memory of her kisses aroused me. I touched myself all over, the way a new lover might. My body felt different, firmer. I liked it. One hand moved to a breast, the other to my thigh. I ran my fingers across my nipples until they got hard. A finger dipped into my opening and was immediately engulfed in satiny wetness. I stroked myself for a long time, unhurriedly, taking pleasure in the peaking and then withdrawing.

Finally I turned over onto my stomach, one hand on my clitoris, the other under my face, and moved until I brought myself to orgasm. As I came and the spasms rocked me, I realized I was biting down on my forearm. I did it again, harder, and it felt great. For good measure, I sucked on the flesh.

Oh, those lips!

special delivery

It was a foggy Sunday afternoon at the height of the San Francisco summer. Cassidy had already finished reading both the *Sunday Chronicle* and the *New York Times,* done three loads of laundry, paid overdue bills, and washed and waxed her car. She had planned to take a hike along the Point Reyes shoreline with her dog, Jessie, but somehow it was already the middle of the afternoon and too late for a long drive.

Cassidy was a single girl. Had been for a while. Her last relationship had lasted two years, a record for her. But the ex-lover had been dependent and domineering, and Cassidy had vowed not to have another repeat. Not for a long time.

It had been months since she'd been with anyone. She was horny as hell. Heck, it had been months since she had even *thought* of sex. But she was thinking about it now, about her first time with Lena.

Dusk at Baker Beach. Two lone fishermen wading in the waves, their lines silver arcs in the air. She and Lena huddled behind a sand dune. The roar of the ocean matched the cadence of her heartbeat. The moon rose, a brilliant white in the indigo sky. She had stared for so long that the image had burned into her retinas.

At first their kisses had been shy, tentative. Then, the months of pent-up energy were released. The tsunami overtook them. One minute they had been kissing awkwardly. Teeth hitting. Embarrassed laughter. The next thing she knew, she was on her stomach, her face on the sand, the taste of the sea in her mouth. The air was startling, like cold water from a shower turned on full force. Somehow, her jeans were halfway down her legs and Lena was on top of her, her fingers working their way expertly, exquisitely, inside.

She groaned, her mouth gritty with sand.

"Yes, yes. Oh, that feels good."

She was so wet she couldn't believe it. Had the ocean somehow defied the laws of nature and traveled uphill, soaking her while she had been preoccupied? But no, it was a wet warmth, familiar and pleasing, like hot cocoa. Lena was rocking on top of her. The weight of her body solid, comforting. Lena's fingers, slick with her juices, slipped out of her and slowly traced the line of her crack. She stiffened.

Lena's fingers stopped, lingered. "You okay?" she whispered into her ear.

Yes, she was okay. She did not want the sensation to end.

"Don't stop. Oh, baby, don't stop. Please don't."

She lay very still then, pressed to the cold sand, her every pore open. Goose bumps spread across her body like wildfire. Lena's mouth was biting her neck, her shoulders. Savage bites, followed by long sucking caresses. Lena's fingers were coaxing her flesh to sing. She was burning down there. Hot. Cold. Nails of ice piercing her flesh. Silken strands caressing her skin. She was afraid. She had never felt like this before. She wanted it. Oh, yes, she wanted to be fucked.

When Lena entered her, she thought she would die from the sheer pleasure of it. Her cries tore the quilt of night. Lena held her tight, stayed inside her, un-moving. The pleasure gathered deep inside, where Lena's fingers rested. But she could restrain herself no longer. Her muscles gripped and strained, moving with their own power.

Finally, she could stand it no longer.

"Fuck me, please, fuck me." The words burst from her lips.

Lena happily complied.

Later, under the moonlight, Cassidy had admired Lena's forearm.

"Thanks for the workout," she had grinned.

"My pleasure," Cassidy grinned back, "and what a pleasure!"

She smiled at the memory. It had been so long since Cassidy had had sex that to say she was ripe for picking and ready for anything was dead on. So what if it was a trite saying, she thought. Stale, flat, as one ex-professor would have said. This was not Creative Writing 101, this was real life!

Newly clean and sober, the idea of going to a bar and cruising was dangerous for her. She considered attending some political event but felt uneasy about pursuing her real agenda in those oh-so-correct situations. At times like these she was jealous of the way gay men had acted in the carefree '70s—with their bathhouses and back rooms for anonymous sex.

Cassidy tried to think of other things to do: work out at the gym, jog in Golden Gate Park with Jessie, have coffee in the Castro, cruise at the Museum of Modern Art, go shopping for things she didn't need and put them on plastic. Or order a pizza with everything on it.

Cassidy decided the latter was her safest bet. Pizza with extra everything. Still, there were so many choices. It was not as simple as sausage or pepperoni, onions or mushrooms anymore. There was feta and cilantro, roasted eggplant and Gruyère cheese, garlic and sundried tomato. Regular, whole wheat, thin crust, deep dish.

She decided on garlic and baby clams, then ordered a large with extra cheese. It didn't matter if she couldn't finish it. She could have cold pizza with coffee for breakfast. Best of all, Jessie didn't mind garlic breath, and she got to eat pizza, too.

The pizza place was true to its ad: the buzzer sounded in fifty minutes. Jessie jumped up and ran to the door, barking as the deliveryman approached cloaked in the heady aroma of pizza. Jessie loved anyone bearing food, even if it was not meant for her. She always got something.

It wasn't until Cassidy pulled money out of her wallet and handed it to the deliveryman that she realized that *he* was a *she*. Tall, broad-shouldered, with square, brown hands. And good-looking to boot.

"Got to be a dyke," she said, half out loud.

"Excuse me?" The woman grinned, showing white, even teeth.

"Uh, nothing." Cassidy turned as red as a beet.

She took the pizza and shut the door in a hurry.

"Did ya get a look at her, Jessie? Woulda liked to have asked her in to eat. Woulda liked to eat her! What would you have done, huh, girl?"

Jessie licked her chops, her tail wagging a mile a minute at the prospect of food.

"I swear, girl, you have no shame. Jessie, I'm talking to you about serious stuff and all you're interested in is food. Okay, hold on. Here, you can have a piece."

Between the two of them, they finished the pizza easily.

"Damn, that was good. I'm stuffed, are you?"

Jessie wagged her tail and whined for more.

"That's it, girl. All gone. Okay, you want more? You call the pizza place and request the same delivery person and I'll spring for another, okay?"

Jessie looked at her mistress and wagged her tail happily.

"Forget it, girl. I know you want more. But I've

had enough. Or have I?"

The next day at work Cassidy couldn't stop thinking about the delivery person. When she got home there were no messages on her machine, something that always made her feel forlorn. After she took Jessie for a romp in the park, she contemplated what to have for dinner. The worst part of living alone was cooking for herself. And damn, she couldn't get the delivery person out of her head.

"No way am I going to eat pizza two nights in a row," she said to Jessie.

Pizza's great every night, Mom, Jessie replied.

Cassidy scanned a stack of take-out menus lazily, as if to trick her true intentions. There was Chinese, barbecue, Italian, Thai, or sushi.

Pizza, Mom. Pizza, urged Jessie, wagging her tail.

"Okay, you've convinced me. What shall we have on it tonight? I know, anything with meat, right?"

You got it, Mom! Oh, and don't forget extra cheese. Skip the garlic though, just in case.

Cassidy remembered that a two-dollar-off coupon had been attached to the previous evening's bill. That was it, a sure sign. She called the pizza place and was put on hold for what seemed like forever. Then she got disconnected.

"I'm not supposed to be doing this. What if it's her night off? What if she has a different route tonight?"

Jessie fixed her with her liquid brown eyes.

Mo-ther!

"Okay, okay. One more try."

This time she was successful in placing her order. Before she hung up she added, "Say, um, the woman who delivered last night, is she working this evening? Oh, okay. Thanks."

Jessie looked up at her mother's crestfallen face.

"Tough luck, kiddo, she's doing special deliveries. Oh, well, it's just you and me, girl. Better luck next time, huh?"

When the doorbell rang, Jessie sprang off her bed, barking.

"Hold on," Cassidy shouted as she went to find her wallet. She was in no hurry. The doorbell rang again.

"Okay, already. You want to be paid or not?"

She opened the door. Jessie ran out between her legs, tail wagging furiously.

"Jessie, get in here. Jessie, come! What do I owe you?"

She started to count out dollar bills. Jessie bumped into her excitedly, and the money fell from her hand. She bent to pick it up. As she stood, she noticed a suspicious bulge in the crotch of the deliveryman's jeans.

Oh, great, she thought, just great. A young jock with a hard-on.

Her eyes went from his crotch to his hands. They were brown and very square. She looked at his face partially hidden under a baseball cap. The delivery person had a grin the size of a basketball.

"Sausage with extra cheese. Skip the garlic. Special delivery."

Oh, yes, Cassidy purred, I love a woman who packs.

"Come on in," she invited. "Come in and help me eat."

sex on-line

You're standing in front of me wearing nothing but your favorite cock. You have my hands bound behind my back. You pull me down onto my knees and gently move my mouth toward you. As I'm sucking you off you start to move your hips back and forth so that you can feel the pressure of the dildo against your clit. When you've decided you want to come, you take off the dildo and let me bring you off with my tongue.

Reading my e-mail that afternoon was a big turn-on. I could hardly wait for seven o'clock. But there was another message.

Can we skip our coffee-by-the-lake ritual after dinner? I want you naked in my bed. I want you inside me. I want you. Can't wait. P.S. Can we skip dinner?

Reply: We can skip coffee by the lake. We cannot skip dinner. *Beware!* You do not want to be around me when I am hungry. I want to be naked in your bed. I want to wrap my arms around you. I want you on your knees. I want my cock in your mouth. I want my fist in your cunt. I want to hear you come. I can't wait. Is it seven o'clock yet?

You tie me spread-eagle on the bed. Straddle my face, the tip of your big cock touching my lips. I whimper at the sight of it. You grab my hair, pull my head up off the bed and push your cock into my mouth.

Reply: I am holding your head in both my hands as I thrust my cock in and out of your mouth. The sight of it is as arousing as the feel of your lips sucking me, pulling me inside you. Oh God, I can't hold on any longer. I'm going to come in your mouth.

. . . .
fantasy number three

I am on my hands and knees. You are positioned behind me, cock at the ready. You push inside me, pump me hard.

Reply: I am fucking you hard and fast. My hands are on your hips, gripping your thighs, pulling you toward me as I thrust in and out. I see your puckered asshole smiling invitation. I slather lube on my thumb and slide it all the way inside.

. . . .
fantasy number four

I am on your lap. Your cock is inside me. I feel the hard muscles in your thighs as you bounce me up and down on your cock.

Reply: I work my hips and thighs, pushing up from the chair. The heels of my boots leave the floor as I thrust inside you.

. . . .
fantasy number five

My hands are handcuffed in front of me. I am leaning over the back of the sofa, my ass in the air. I hear you take off your belt, wrap it around your fist. The leather slices the air. I feel the sting on my cheeks.

Reply: I am coming over. Right now.

the abduction of Shar

When we pulled up to the brownstone on Byron, snow began to fall. J.D. cut the headlights immediately. I got out of the car and pulled my cashmere scarf tighter around my neck though I left my leather coat unbuttoned. I looked up at her window and saw in the glow of the streetlight hundreds of falling snowflakes shining like stars.

The maid let us into the apartment.

"The Mistress is in her dressing room, Sir. Please take cocktails in the West Room."

There was a huge fire going in the fireplace. J.D. mixed me my usual, Coke, no ice, with a splash of Rose's lime juice. I stood by the windows looking out into the street. The snowflakes were larger now, the size of cotton puffs. I smiled. By the time I was finished with Shar tonight, Chicago would be under five feet of snow.

I met Shar at OutWrite, a gay and lesbian writer's conference in Boston two years ago. I'm an editor with a small trade house and Shar's a playwright. I was falling asleep listening to two very dull authors speaking on a panel when I felt a hand on my shoulder.

"I'll let you know if you begin to snore," a voice said. "Save you the embarrassment."

Utterly embarrassed, I turned around. A woman with a shaved head, jade green eyes, and a wicked grin sat behind me. Her hand remained on my shoulder.

It's shallow, all right, I have to admit. I can't explain it, but I love women who wear glasses, though I myself have twenty-twenty vision. In the sixties it was wire-rimmed octagonals tinted green. In the seventies it was granny glasses. Aviators in the eighties and L.A. Eyeworks now. She was wearing a pair of oval Giorgio Armani's. And she was falling asleep in the seat in front of mine.

"Shar," she said, "pleased to make your acquaintance."

"Locke," I replied, without missing a beat, "accent on the *e*."

"Since I see you're not taking notes, want to go have some lunch before it gets crowded?"

"Yes," I nodded, "I think I would."

The hotel dining room was already packed, so when she suggested we go to her suite and order from room service, I smiled my assent.

I don't remember the meal, but the afternoon was unforgettable.

Beginning with the strawberries. A bowl full of ripe berries, bright red, almost crimson. The room redolent with their scent. Shar took one in her fingers, dipped it into a bowl of sour cream, and offered it to me. The strawberry tasted like the berries I remember from my childhood—heavy, fragrant, and bursting with flavor. The next thing I knew, her fingers were in my mouth and mine were unzipping her dress. As I unhooked her bra, it got tangled in my watchband and around my wrist so when I finally fucked her with my hand, the black lace and elastic gripped me like a vise.

I bore the mark of it for a week.

Like most people, I keep the pleasant memories close to the surface; the bad ones get buried deep.

Shar swept into the room, resplendent in a black backless evening dress, opera-length gloves, and high heels. Her eyebrows and head looked freshly shaved and her face was free of makeup. Her cheekbones were high and her eyes almost unnaturally slanted, like those of a Chinese opera singer. Five diamond studs sparkled in her right ear.

"Darling," she said as she approached. "How good to see you."

I rose to greet her. J.D. remained on the floor by my feet.

"Drink?" I asked.

"Yes, that would be nice."

J.D. immediately got up and went to the bar.

I talked about a book I had just acquired, a first novel by a popular performance artist.

"It has a story line, I hope. Or are sentences and paragraphs too concrete for conceptual artists?"

I laughed.

"The book is daring in its subject matter and the language is—well, shall we just say that the words will challenge even the most severe critic of form."

I looked at her sitting on the sofa, backlit by the flames. The wine, or perhaps the fire, had brought a flush to her cheeks, faint brush strokes on a white canvas.

"Enough chitchat, my dear. I think it is time for us to begin the evening."

J.D. appeared at my side with something in her hand.

"Shar," I beckoned.

She came and knelt on the carpet in front of me. I reached out and took her head in my hands, stroked the smoothness of her skull. I felt heat gathering in my crotch, warmth spreading up to my solar plexus. There is something very sexual about a woman's naked head. I took the leather hood from J.D. and as I slipped it over Shar's head, I heard the sharp hiss of her breath.

The fruity bouquet of the Merlot lingered in my mouth. When Locke drew the hood over my head, the smell of leather engulfed my senses. My world went black.

Under J.D.'s sure hands, the car shot through the night, its wipers working at high speed to clear the snow. There was virtually no traffic on the road, and snowplows had already preceded us on Lakeshore Drive.

Shar lay in my arms, relaxed but alert while I stroked her hooded head absently.

There are no eye holes or detachable mouthpiece in this hood, only ventilation slits by the nostrils. I am in Locke's arms where I know I am safe. I can feel her heart next to me. I hear nothing. I see nothing. Her hands are caressing my head, and I feel a sudden gush of emotion as tears flood my eyes.

My best friend, Anita, lay in a hospital bed for weeks consumed by pain. The cancer and the chemo had stripped her of her hair, her flesh, her dignity, and her will. I traced her cracked lips with a piece of ice, sang our silly childhood ditties, and read poetry to her while tears streamed down my face. She no longer had a voice. She could no longer see me. I stroked her head. The down was as soft as a baby's first growth of hair.

On the day she died, I went to a barber to have my head shaved. It's been two years since her death, and I've worn it like this ever since.

This will be Shar's first time in a dungeon, and I'm determined to make it good. She is sobbing quietly in my arms so I take off the hood—warning her to keep her eyes closed—to make sure she's all right.

She insists she is.

It is just before the witching hour and we make

quite an entrance at the play party. I am in full leather, as is J.D., who is carrying the hooded Shar in her arms. Other tops nod at me as we pass. Bottoms, men and women both, genuflect in their different ways. One woman I see frequently blows me a kiss but I do not return her greeting.

J.D. carries Shar right to the rack where a couple are finishing up.

"I'm going to take the hood off so keep your eyes closed for a bit while they adjust to the light," I warn.

She nods her head.

J.D. takes a flogger out of the toy bag and hands it to me. The strands of leather are a foot and a half long, red and black.

"I know this is your first time, so I'll start gently. Remember what we discussed earlier?"

Shar nods again.

"We'll go slow. And remember to use your safe word if you need to. All right?"

"Yes...Sir," she adds uncertainly.

J.D. ties Shar to the rack. I unbutton my leather shirt.

I feel naked. Truth is, I feel a little silly. Here I am in my black dress and opera gloves, stretched, no tied, to some kind of a rack. The light is dim in here, but people are looking at me. I can sense it. I feel naked. What am I doing here?

Suddenly a rush of air and *thup,* a jolt as the leather strands connect with my back. Then light sweeps, gentle, caressing. The air breezes against me. It is sensuous, cooling. I am smiling, thinking, this feels wonderful, like leather kisses, leather wind, leather rain. What was I afraid of? Why would one need to use a safe word, when out of the blue, a force knocks the breath out of me. Again and again. Alternately left side, right side, left, right. The heavy thud of leather, then the mean sting of a different whip, I think, one with thin strands. I am shocked into submission. Then there is nothing. Suddenly I am heaving, sucking air like a drowning woman. I feel heat rising from my flesh. Cool hands on my back. A voice in my ear: "Darling, how do you feel?"

Her back is red and streaked with welts that are already beginning to darken. She feels hot to my touch. I motion to J.D. to release her. She falls into my arms. Her cheeks are wet. I kiss her face. There is something about wielding a whip that makes my blood boil. I am so wet I think I could come right here and now. But there is someone else I must think of.

"Darling, how do you feel?"

My body is warm. I feel like a of piece of coal that's glowing. My cunt is very wet. I know it.

J.D. leads Shar to an empty sling, settles her gently back into it and ties her feet up in the straps. I pull on a latex glove and spread lube over my hand. I bend over Shar, who is spread out in front of me. I smell the scent of her desire, strong and enticing. I want to take her in my mouth, all of her, dental dams be damned. Instead, I rub my nose in her wetness and content myself with teasing her clit.

She moans. "Please, please—"

"What do you want, my darling?"

"I want you to come inside me. Oh, please, I can't stand it any longer."

"Then ask properly."

"Please, oh, please—Please, Sir, come inside me. Please," she begs. "Please, Sir, please. Oh, I need it."

She is shaking, weeping.

I bend over and kiss her. Softly, gently, savoring

her mouth as I might savor a piece of rare filet mignon.
I suck her tongue deep into my mouth.

"Hold her," I instruct J.D., "hold her and stroke
her while I fist her."

She is so wet I almost don't need the lube. I insert
two fingers, then three, and four. In and out. I nudge
slowly, steadily, patiently, until my knuckles are straining to push past her resistance.

I feel like I am on fire down there. I want to take
all of Locke inside me and yet can I? I'm on fire, burning, flames in my cunt, blazing down my legs, scorch-
ing my toes.

She is so tight. I feel if I force my fist inside her, I
will harm her. I swivel my fist, gently, oh, so gently.
With my other hand I find her clitoris. It is hard and
greedy. "Rub me, rub me," she moans. "Yes, please,"
she begs. I rub her hard and fast, turning my fist one
way then the other, and all in a rush, she opens, opens
to take me in. I slide my fist all the way inside her, my
euphoria rising like a glorious erection.

I love fucking with my fist. I fucking love it. My
whole being is inside her, pounding her, loving her.

I feel her gripping my fist and I am ready to come,
too. I look up and see that J.D. is locking lips with her,
her hands on her head, her smooth, shaved head.

Do you know what it's like to be fisted and kissed
at the same time? The only thing better is having one
woman go down on you while another woman is kissing you on the mouth. Do you know what it's like?

Of course, Locke's the best, and J.D.'s training
with her, so the two of them together is like nothing on
earth.

Do you know what it's like?

the girl loves garlic

It actually happened to me. One night I went to bed with a lover and things were fine. We had a house with a white picket fence (well, a condo in a high-rise), a dog, two cars, food in the refrigerator, money in the bank. The next morning, everything had changed.

I'm a writer who had just spent the last two years finishing a novel. I had gone to bed the previous night, as I usually did, with my lover and my dog. Life felt solid. Stable. The next morning Girlfriend confronted me with everything she had been unhappy about for the past two years, and then some.

She told me that the sex sucked. Said that I wasn't her friend, that I was distant and detached. Emotionally bankrupt. She said she got pissed every time I asked her to turn the TV down while I was working. She's been pissed about the TV for two years and she's telling me now?

She told me I wasn't meeting her needs. She hadn't been meeting mine for some time either, but I was focused on my book.

"My writing will always come first," I made the mistake of saying.

"I'm not sure we can work it out," she said. "It might be too late."

"Too late?"

How could it be too late? This is the first time she's brought it up. Oh, did I mention that Girlfriend and I got married three years ago on Gay Day? I thought this was a committed relationship. I thought I was going to have children with this woman. I thought we were going to grow old together. I thought this was for forever. And she's talking about it being too late?

She admitted that she had been dissatisfied for months but wanted to try to resolve it herself to spare me the possible pain. Oh, spare me. Is she in a relationship by herself? Oh, did I mention Girlfriend is a therapist?

She told me she got so used to my involvement with my writing, to not being there, that to her I am no longer here.

I can tell you I was in a state of shock. It felt like someone hit me over the head with a baseball bat. Girlfriend was not talking about a-marriage-gone-wrong-and-could-we-change-and-make-it-better. She was saying it was bad and it was over. Period. Finito. Full stop.

I went to bed one night with my lover and my dog and everything was fine. When I woke up the next day, someone hit me with a baseball bat.

So now I'm alone—me and my dog, that is. I hurt. I cry at times. I'm not rational. I'll be driving my car and all of a sudden fierce emotion grips me and hot tears run down my cheeks. And, of course, I think, What did I do wrong? Was I that bad? My close friends gently remind me, "You know what a bitch you can be." Was it me? Was it my fault?

Only one good thing came out of this mess. Garlic.

I love garlic. Girlfriend didn't. Or, as she would say, she liked it but it didn't like her. Whenever I ate garlic I would have to brush my teeth twice, gargle with mouthwash, chew gum, suck on a Certs, and sit across the room from her. When I hugged her, careful to keep my mouth averted, she would say, "Garlic."

I love to eat garlic. Raw slivers on a turkey sandwich, roasted cloves spread on a baguette, fried in olive oil, pureed in guacamole, sprinkled on popcorn. I love the smell of garlic on my fingers, the scent of it in the air, the taste of it in my mouth, on my tongue.

Now that I'm single I can eat garlic anytime I want. In my omelet, on fried rice, boiled in soup. My dog doesn't mind garlic at all.

Last night I went to bed alone and snuggled up to my dog. The house smelled like chicken and roasted garlic. I smiled as I floated off into dreams.

I am hugging a woman. Her warm breath brushes my ear.

"Come closer," she says, "I want to give you pleasure like you've never experienced."

Her hands travel down my flanks, her touch gentle as falling petals.

She leans toward me and kisses me tentatively at first, then with urgency and great force. Her hair falls into my face, tickling me. I try to pull away but a firm hand cups the back of my neck and forces me to heed her will as her tongue explores the cavern of my mouth.

My hands are touching her breasts, squeezing the nipples. She moans and allows me to draw my mouth away from hers so I can suckle her breasts. I nuzzle my nose in her armpits, smell her sweat, lick the hairs that grow there thick in the hollow. I move down, down, over her round stomach and find myself between her legs, where the unmistakable aroma of garlic greets me.

I open her legs, push my fingers into her tangle of dark hair. Her clitoris rises to meet my hand, hard and tough, like a clove of garlic. I sink down to her, mouth open, tongue ready. I grip her with my mouth, massage her clit with my lips. I bite into her with my teeth, drawing blood. The metallic tang of it fills my senses. Pleasure sweeps over me as the sharp taste of garlic explodes in my mouth.

Oh, yes.

the cutting

When Brooke first came out into the scene almost a decade ago, there were many things she thought were plain revolting: piercing—temporary and permanent—branding, canes, water sports, scat, and cutting.

She had a friend who very much enjoyed being cut. Her friend sported the scars proudly all over her body. One day she held a cutting party. Brooke politely declined. But when the night came Brooke was alone. Her date for the evening had canceled, so she went to the party for food, drink, and the company.

When it was time for the cutting to begin, Brooke positioned herself in the front row, much to her surprise. As the scalpel cut into the woman's flesh and blood seeped from the thin lines drawn on her skin, Brooke's eyes never left her back. Throughout the two-hour-long process, Brooke was spellbound. And from that moment on, she was hooked.

Beginning a couple of years after that, Brooke actively searched for someone to do a cutting on her. But somehow it had never worked out. Until she met Adrian.

It was Adrian's forty-second birthday and a party had been thrown in her honor. Brooke went with a mutual friend. When Adrian and Brooke were introduced, a current shot through Brooke's body. They held on to each other's hand for what seemed like a long time. When Adrian walked away to greet her other guests, Brooke watched her. She wore a white shirt, black pants, and boots. Her bearing was erect, her stride sure.

Brooke watched her all night long. The silver in her dark hair caught the light. She moved with an easy confidence, and her laughter carried across the room, brushing Brooke's ears like silk.

The next evening they went to dinner at a Chinese restaurant. After they had finished eating and were opening their fortune cookies, Brooke asked: "So, Adrian, Susan told me you were interested in playing? Is that correct?"

That's something Brooke loved about leatherwomen. They put it right out there. No dicking around or beating around the bush. *Want to play? Yes. When? How about now? Sure. Want to fuck? Yes. Got gloves and lube? Great.* Vanilla girls could learn a few things.

"Yes," she replied without hesitation. "I am."

So they did.

On the first date they did a flogging scene. The next night Brooke got a combo. Adrian gave her a great massage and one of the best fucks she'd ever experienced. The night after that, Adrian did a cutting on her.

"You're an experienced player, and very popular it seems. Why choose me to do it?" Adrian asked.

"I've wanted it for a long time," Brooke responded, "but I've never met the right person. I feel connected to you. I want to know what it feels like. I want it to be with you but I can't explain why."

"Why do you want a cutting?" Adrian continued.

"I have a fascination with sharp edges. Swords, switchblades, straight razors. I've played with knives, but not when they've broken the skin. I want to experience it. I want to know what the sensation's like. And I love the taste of blood. You don't know how much I loved eating out a woman who was bleeding."

"Umm, yes, I miss that too. In fact I miss going down on a woman, period. I can do without the experience of dental dams."

"Yeah. I haven't eaten pussy in years. I hate latex, so I just don't do it at all."

"More's the pity." Adrian touched her arm. "Well, my dear, here's your chance to taste blood again. There's nothing safer than your own."

She lay Brooke down on the bed and kissed her. Adrian's tongue moved into her mouth and she sucked, savored it as if it were treacle.

"Just remember to keep breathing," she whispered. "I'm right here with you."

Adrian covered both her hands with latex gloves. When she removed the scalpel from its wrapping, Brooke held her breath. Adrian brought the light closer, leaned over, and smiled.

"Adrian, I'm scared," Brooke said.

"Yes, and so you should be. A blade is a dangerous thing."

The edge of it touched Brooke's skin. It felt like a pointed pencil until Adrian pressed down and Brooke drew in a sharp breath. The experience was neither a burning sensation nor an icy pain. There was an intensity to the sensation that defied description.

Adrian drew the Chinese character for *love* on Brooke's left breast. In blood. Four strokes that she re-cut four times. Then she brought out a switchblade, scraped up the blood, and placed the edge of it on Brooke's tongue. The blood tasted metallic. She wanted more.

"Make me bleed again. Please," Brooke begged.

"I think that's enough for your first time," Adrian said firmly, a smile playing on her lips. "If I didn't know you were a top, I'd accuse you of being a greedy bottom."

"Right now that's exactly how I feel."

"Good. I hope you feel like a masochist too because I'm about to pour alcohol on it."

The coldness of the rubbing alcohol combined with the stinging heat when it hit Brooke's flesh gave her a jolt. It was definitely a combination of pain and pleasure.

"Will it scar?"

"Probably not this time. But if I recut it after it's healed it might."

"I want the mark of it to be permanent. It's my first and I want to keep it. I want to keep something from you," Brooke added shyly.

"I could rub salt on it."

"Salt! Are you kidding?"

"No, I take my play very seriously, but I'd have to tie you down first."

Salt! And the woman's not kidding? What am I do-ing in her bed? a voice in Brooke's head screamed. *Get out of here. Get out right away.*

"Ah, I see that scared you, didn't it? The thought of me rubbing salt into your open cuts. Why don't you just anticipate that then. I'll do you when you heal. I'll recut you and then rub salt into your skin. Frighten-ing, isn't it? But I bet you're wet just thinking about it. Aren't you?"

Brooke nodded her head. She had been wet for some time, gloriously wet.

Adrian put down the scalpel. Her latex-clad hand traveled down Brooke's body. She found her wetness and plunged inside. Then pulled out and went in search of her clit.

"Are you breathing?" she asked. "Oh, you're swol-len and so hard."

"Adrian, Adrian," Brooke moaned, "if you keep touching me there I'm going to come."

"Not without asking you're not."

"Oh, I can't, I can't hold on much longer."

"Then ask. Say my name and ask for permission."

"Adrian..."

"Yes?"

"I...I'm going to come. Oh, Adrian, can I? Can I come?"

She rubbed Brooke harder, faster.

"Yes, yes. Come for me now."

As the contractions gripped her, Brooke called out her name. "AdrianAdrianAdrianAdrianAdrian."

Later that week, Brooke made a journal entry:

"I'm back at home now. Adrian and I live in different cities. But I bear the mark of her still.

Love, on my breast."

a little tenderness

She lay on the bed, the T-shirt stretched taut across her chest, drinking in with all her senses the caress of the other woman's hand, tender as a shower of petals. It had been so long, so long since a woman had touched her with love.

Then the hand moved from the plain of her stomach and traced the line of the sternum up to the rise of her breasts. Tenderly the hand stroked the soft cotton. She shivered involuntarily. A gasp caught in her throat as she felt her nipples rise and harden in response to the woman's touch.

"I've missed you," she whispered.

The hand stopped, its weight suddenly heavy, a stone on her breast.

"Sorry. I guess what I meant to say is that I've missed having a lover. I've missed being touched and held."

"How long has it been?"

The hand resumed its caressing.

"We broke up almost a year ago. We were together for five," she said slowly, "but I think it was probably three years before the relationship ended that we stopped making love."

"Three years, and one year alone. That's a long time. Too long to be without love."

The woman's hand slipped under the elastic of her shorts, encountering flesh for the first time.

She moaned as fingers moved down her navel, to the wings of the pelvic bone, then slid in the crease where her upper thigh joined the groin. She jerked suddenly, as if awakened from a dream.

"What's the matter?" the woman asked.

"Oh, I'm sorry, I don't know. Sorry—I should stop saying sorry. Guess maybe I'm not ready yet."

"That's okay. I like you, you should know that by now. We've been friends for six months. I want to get to know you better. I want to get close to you, but I'm not in any hurry."

The woman withdrew her hand from underneath the shorts and laid it gently on the other woman's stomach.

"It's just that you're so tender..."

The words trailed off as if they were too painful to speak.

"It's like earlier when you stroked my head, I felt like crying. I haven't felt gentleness for so long. Julie, she was so rough, uncaring. Even when we made love, I felt like I had no body. She would go right between my legs, kiss me a little there, then shove her fingers inside. That would be it. Sometimes I felt like one of those blow-up dolls, a hole surrounded by pubic hair. It was as if I had no legs, no arms, no breasts, no back, no body at all. I was just a handy orifice. She hardly ever kissed me. She never held my hand. She never even called me by name, only when she was angry and being sarcastic."

She began to cry.

"Oh, Kelly, I'm so sorry. What can I do for you?"

"Just take me in your arms. Hold me, please."

Kelly lay in the circle of Gina's arms and cried, the tears landing on Gina's skin like melting snowflakes.

"Oh, I'm sorry. Here I invited you over for dinner and a video and I'm balling my eyes out. Oh, God, I said sorry again. Sorry." And she burst out laughing.

Gina began to laugh with her. They rolled apart,

laughing, holding their stomachs.

"That feels better."

"Which," asked Gina, "the crying or the laughing part?"

"Both." And Kelly burst into another flurry of laughter, showering spittle on her friend. "Oops, sorry. Oh, I did it again!" And she collapsed into yet another gale, a hand over her mouth.

Finally, Kelly reached over and wiped Gina's cheek with her hand.

"There. What should we call that? A nonconsensual exchange of bodily fluids?" She giggled.

"Not exactly. It was only yours, so it wasn't an exchange. How about a consensual one now?" She grinned.

Kelly looked at the woman in front of her. Gina wore her dark hair long down her back. Her grin was girlish, but crow's feet branched from her eyes and lines rimmed her mouth.

"Yes," she replied, as she moved in closer for a kiss.

Their mouths connected and held. Gina felt Kelly's heat. She pushed her tongue inside Kelly's mouth and Kelly sucked it in, greedy as a newly initiated bottom, hungry for every sensation.

Gina trailed her hand down Kelly's broad back, cupped one cheek and stroked her.

Kelly broke away from the kiss, moaning.

"Ooh, ooh. I love to be touched. Touch me everywhere. I want to feel your hands all over my body."

She disentangled herself from Gina and pulled off her T-shirt and shorts, exposing her body for the first time.

"Kelly," Gina breathed, taking in the sight of her. "You're so beautiful."

"You really think so?"

"Yes, absolutely." She ran her hand down Kelly's arm, over the rise of a hip, and rested it on her thigh. "Yes, I think you're gorgeous."

"Julie never said that to me."

"What was wrong with that woman? She must have had blinders over her eyes."

"I felt so unattractive. And our sex life was so seldom, so sparse and quick, I began to feel undesirable too. Asexual even."

"Kelly," Gina said, looking into her eyes, "look at me. This is Gina here, not Julie. That part of your life is over, and from all that you've told me, it's surely for the best. Julie sounds like a dud, a real bore."

"Yes, yes, I guess, but I didn't fall in love with her because she was a party girl. That's not what I wanted. I wasn't looking for excitement or drama. I'd had enough of that when I was younger, believe me. I'm kind of a homebody. But just once in a while I'd like to go out to a club, take in an art opening, or do something fun and unusual. She never wanted to do anything but go shopping at Marshall Field's, or to the movies. I haven't been dancing in five years for God's sake."

"You haven't?"

Kelly shook her head.

"We can fix that. Come on."

"Where? I'm not dressed."

"You don't have to be. Come on, get up."

Gina got off the bed and padded to the stereo in her bare feet.

"Oh, wait. Before I do that, where are your matches? I want to light some candles."

Gina switched off the light and pushed the play button on the CD player. Anita Baker's voice filled the room.

Ain't there something I can give to you
In exchange for everything you give to me?

Gina turned to her, smiled and offered her hand. Kelly stood up, proud in her body, and stepped into Gina's embrace, nestling easily into the taller woman.

We love so strong and so unselfishly
And I made a vow so I tell you now
I'm giving you the best that I got, baby...

"I'm giving you the best that I got, Kelly," Gina sang along.

When Kelly heard Gina singing her name out loud, something inside her melted. She turned her head up for a kiss.

Before the song faded, Gina led her to the bed. She caressed Kelly all over her body, from her neck to her toes. Then she planted kisses from the backs of her knees to her shoulder blades.

"Oh, Gina," Kelly sighed, "I'm wet. I was never wet with—"

"Shh, no more saying her name, okay? Let me touch you and see. Oh, yes, you are so very wet."

As Gina stroked her labia apart, marveling at the satin wetness, she could bear it no longer.

"I have to taste you. Oh, Kelly, let me eat you."

Without waiting for a reply, she slid down the length of Kelly's legs and took her full in her mouth. The woman smell filled her senses, intoxicating her. Grabbing both cheeks of Kelly's ass, she lifted her closer and licked and sucked and reveled in the scent of a woman. Of Kelly.

Kelly felt the orgasm shake her to the tips of her toes. It surged and spun, gathered, and surged again. As the orgasms gripped her, her mouth opened and she screamed. "Giiiiina!"

"Here I am, Kelly."

Gina wiped her face on the sheet beneath Kelly's legs, and pulled herself up to cover her friend.

"I'm here, Kelly, I'm here for you. I'm here with you."

Kelly was heaving from the intensity of the climaxes. Suddenly, she burst into tears. They gushed out of her, as fierce as the contractions in her vagina.

"It's okay, Kelly, let it out. Let it all out. I'm here, Kelly. We're here together, and everything is all right for now. I promise."

Kelly cried. It had been so long since someone had said her name. It had been so long since someone cared. It had been so long since she had been touched. It had been so long since she had been shown a little tenderness.

Dear Daddy and Doña: One of my fantasies is being fucked by two tops. Are the both of you up for it? Another fantasy is being tied to a tree and getting flogged. Love, boy nigel.

Dear boy nigel: Let's get a little more specific, shall we? Daddy loves little boys' asses, while Doña loves their big cunts. Do you like dildos or fingers or fists? Doña also loves to chew on nipples and shoulders. And we're both oh so fond of canes and fire. How do you like it? One or the other orifice, both at once, or one and then the other? How do you like it? Leaning up against a tree, or on your hands and knees, spread and dripping? Or on your back, with four strong women holding you down? Tell us more. D & D.

Dear Daddy and Doña: Thank you for your letter which I read with great glee. This boy will try to answer your questions. I love dildos, fingers, and fists, though I'm afraid of both canes and fire. Everything else that you suggested sounds wonderful too. My fantasy involves being fucked in front by Doña and from behind by Daddy. I will write more later. I am not feeling very well today but I wanted to get back to you right away. My chiropractor said that my soul is emerging and that causes nausea. Love, boy nigel.

Dear boy nigel: Sorry that you are feeling nauseous, but it seems a good thing for your soul to emerge from the shell of pain you seem to have been inhabiting. As for your fantasy, let us be more direct: Daddy and Doña want *details*. To put it another way, you get what you ask for. Or to use a cliché: the squeaky wheel gets the oil. };> Waiting, D & D.

P.S. And speaking of fear. Fear is a good thing. Fear can be very, hmm, fun. The physical sensations that signal fear are very similar (and often the same) to those that signal sexual arousal. Mixing the two so that they become inseparable and/or using one to increase the other is one of the things D & D *really* like to do.

Dear Daddy and Doña: *Sorry* I haven't replied sooner but now that I've put it out there to the universe, I'm frightened. But, Sir and Madame, this boy has been well-trained so here goes:

I would like to be collared and tied to a tree. A tree with the *roughest* bark, please. I would like to be flogged on my back. Please, Sir and Madame, as hard as you can give it to me. Doña, I have small nipples and big shoulders. I would be honored if you would chew on them. Later I would like to have my briefs cut off me. I know you're both fond of canes and I will try to endure as you indulge yourselves on my ass and thighs. Excuse me, Sir and Madame, but I don't know how you are planning on playing with fire. Suffice it to say that this boy will trust himself to the flames in your able hands. I will have my boy simon, and he will take care of me and clean me up for your further pleasure. I would like Doña to fuck me in my cunt and Daddy to fuck me in my ass. *Please, Sir*, please be gentle at first as this boy has had neither a cock nor even a finger up his ass for the last three years. After you have both used me for your pleasure, I will have my boy clean me up. Then I will kiss your boots in gratitude. If you wish me to perform any other duty, I would be most glad to do so to the best of my ability. In closing, Sir and Madame, please know that if boy simon is needed for anything, he is also at your service. I remain, faithfully, boy nigel.

Good boy! We know that it is often hard to ask for what you want and you are to be commended on working through your fear and putting it out there. D & D

P.S. Hello, boy nigel, Daddy here. Of course I will be tender with your sweet ass. I shall have to give you extra attention. Three years without is much too long. Following are some instructions. For your future reference, when Daddy gives directions, he gives them only once, so listen:

Buy a small butt plug. If you can find one that's black or red, that's best. Black is the first choice, red follows, and then anything other than that "flesh" color. Of course, if that's all you can find...

Second. Get a hair cut. Make sure that your clothes are pressed and your boots spit-shined. *Always* be perfectly presentable.

Third. Spend every moment on the drive up in anticipation.

Dear Randy and Amber: Hey, listen you guys, I just got your last e-mail about final festival preparations and I'm *freaking* big time. Then I went and reread boy nigel's e-mail to you (yeah, the one that starts with being collared and tied to a tree) and now I'm really freaking. Did I say that? Did I actually write that and send it out on-line? What am I, nuts?! =:{ I gotta be. First of all, I've never *never* worn a collar. I'm petrified of canes. I mean, they fucking *hurt*. And to top it off, I'm afraid of fire. And to top that, to ask Daddy to ream my butt, I must be mad. Daddy has a big cock. Daddy has a huge cock and I was *not* joking when I said I haven't had anything up my ass for three years. Okay, I gotta rethink this. And the more I think about it, the more I think I *am* nuts and I better just call it off. Hey, I'm not afraid of losing face. I'd rather lose face than lose my hide. You got that right. Never mind negotiation, let's just forget it. Really, you guys, let's forget I mentioned anything, okay? I must have been out of my mind. I must have been on an endorphin high. Okay, so now that I'm sane, just forget it. Signed, Kate. P.S. I'm serious, okay? P.P.S. Dead serious.

Dear boy nigel: Quit your ranting and raving and sit down. *Now.* Place your feet flat on the floor and put your hands in your lap. Close your eyes. Breathe in and out slowly. Breathe deep into your chest. As you exhale, let it out with a sound. Count your breaths. Do not think. When you arrive at the count of one hundred, get up and lay out your clothes and boots. Keep breathing. Dress yourself carefully. Go stand in front of the mirror. See yourself through Daddy and Doña's eyes. Trust us. Know that we will take good care of our boy. Put yourself into our hands.

Open yourself to adventure. The universe awaits.

We will see you in the Twilight Zone at Michigan.

Come prepared.

Come dressed.

Come.

the foodie club

Artichokes. Fresh artichokes with mayonnaise or bottled hearts packed in oil, garlic, and herbs. Which should she choose for the picnic that had been planned? She was about to be initiated into the Foodie Club, and it would be a major catastrophe if anything went wrong.

Shit. She was so nervous she could barely think straight. Should she prepare fresh artichokes they could eat with their hands, or should she make a chicken dish with sour cream, mushrooms, and bottled hearts? Too messy. Maybe she should just drive to Le Poulet and pick up something to go. No, that would be cheating and any bona fide member of the Foodie Club would see right through it.

When she was growing up they had store-bought potato salad and coleslaw, hotdogs and chips. On occasion they ate hamburgers mixed with packets of onion soup for seasoning and oatmeal to stretch the meat. When grilled and slathered with ketchup, the burgers tasted okay.

But this was a different ball game. This was the Foodie Club.

A dozen long-stemmed red roses. Or should they be yellow? Yellow for friendship. Red for love. Better do yellow for the time being. Not the crystal vase. It would be too heavy to maneuver. The glass one would have to do. Candles in the silver candlesticks would be a nice touch. Yes. Cloth napkins, ironed, of course. Matching placemats. Wooden napkin rings. Two wine glasses. Silverware. No plastic forks and knives for her picnic. No indeed.

As for the menu, she had put a lot of thought into it. She would prepare lime-caper chicken and a new potato salad—fresh peas, garlic, and a dribble of virgin olive oil.

Or perhaps, she hesitated, she should make different kinds of finger food. Wouldn't that be easier? No. Lime-caper chicken was one of her best dishes, and it tasted delicious hot or cold.

She removed the chicken breasts from the refrigerator, laid them on the chopping board, and picked up the poultry shears. While she meticulously skinned and deboned the breasts, she recalled last week's phone conversation with Helene.

"Back home I have a group of friends who all love to eat. We'd get together once a week and try a new restaurant or go to one of our homes for a meal. And, of course, every holiday was an occasion to cook."

"Ooh, that sounds great. What's your favorite holiday meal?"

"That's hard, I like them all. But probably Thanksgiving. I love to make turkey with all the trimmings. In fact, the first year I moved away, Annie called me long distance to get step-by-step instructions on the entire menu. One Thanksgiving it was at Annie's and she overcooked the turkey. There is nothing I loathe so much as overcooked white meat. Poor Annie, she never heard the end of it! She refused to do Thanksgiving at her place again. Until I moved away."

"Do you miss it? Home, I mean."

"Yes, I miss my friends. It's so hard to meet people in this city. That's why I answered your ad in the paper."

"Yes, it *is* hard. Even for me, and I've lived here all

my life. I broke up with my lover months ago but I wasn't ready to start dating until now. I put the ad in the paper on a dare, actually. That's how two really good friends of mine, Jo and Michele, got together, and they dared me to place an ad, too. Come to think of it, I know four or five lesbian couples who met that way. Jim and Scotty also. So here you and I are!"

"Yes, here we are."

"Tell me, what drew you to my ad?"

"Are you kidding? The line about food, of course. If you hadn't gathered from our previous conversations, I'm a foodie with a capital *F.*"

Helene's laughter trilled across the telephone lines. "Ah, yes, of course. But how did you know it referred to food? 'Loves to eat' could mean any number of things."

"Yes, and I intended to find out."

She laughed again. It was a very pleasant sound to Lindy's ears.

"How did you get the name Lindy?"

"I was born Linda Ann but I hated it. I was always a tomboy, or at least as far back as I can remember. Lindy was my childhood name and I kept it."

"So," Helene hesitated for a long moment, "how should we plan our date?"

"I think we should do a night at the Palmer House Hilton."

"That sounds great. Do we get to order room service for every meal?"

"No, I think we should each plan to bring something for dinner. You know, like going on a picnic. Except that we would be picnicking in a hotel room."

"That sounds different."

"It'll be fun. And since neither of us drinks, we can empty out the liquor from the fridge and use that for any perishables."

Helene laughed. "I can't remember the last time I

heard someone use that word."

"Which word?"

"Perishables."

"Oh." Lindy paused. "Are you laughing at me?"

"No, of course not. I just think it's a funny word."

"Well, what do you think? We'll form a foodie club of our own. The first meeting of the Foodie Club at the Palmer House Hilton. Two makes it a quorum. Does it sound like a plan?"

"Oh, yes. Absolutely."

Helene sat at the kitchen table with a cup of tea, paging through her roommate's copy of the *New York Times Cookbook*. There were too many choices. Appetizers. Soups. Meats. Poultry. Fish and Shellfish. Eggs, Cheese, Rice and Pasta. And that was just the first page of the Contents. She'd grown up on macaroni and cheese, tuna casseroles and Spaghetti-Os. Now she was supposed to whip up something to serve to a self-professed foodie. Perhaps she should just take the butcher knife and slit her wrists.

The book fell open to a recipe for roast beef, high-temperature method. There was nothing she enjoyed better than a thick piece of prime rib, bloody rare. She suddenly caught herself. What was she thinking? There was no way she was going to take a slab of cold beef to their rendezvous at the Palmer House. No way in the world.

She tossed the book onto the table in disgust. A newspaper clipping fell out. "Rx: 2 lab-tested chicken soups." Oh, sure, I'll bring a pot of soup, Helene thought. On the other side was a recipe for marinated beef salad. Interesting, she thought, as she read. Rare prime rib with two kinds of peppers, scallions, snow peas, and toasted sesame seeds. The recipe looked easy, and it sounded exotic, something a foodie would be sure to appreciate. Why not? Helene thought. I was daring enough to put the ad in the paper in the first place. I can try my hand at this dish.

The poultry scissors cut through bone, cartilage, and flesh as if they were paper. Lindy arranged two large breasts in a glass baking dish and poured a mixture of lime juice, capers, and olive oil over them. She left them to marinate while she cleaned tiny new potatoes, shelled peas, and chopped garlic.

Lindy was nervous about the date. She and Helene had met only four times, and this would be their first time to "do it." They had had many phone conversations to negotiate the matter of sex. Both had wanted to meet on neutral ground—at a hotel. But now that the big day had arrived, she was as nervous as she had been the night the prom queen kissed her in the back of her daddy's car. That had been some night.

"Jeanne, what are you doing here? Where's Hal?"

"Hal? That big, handsome, hunky football hero who took me to the prom?" Jeanne tossed her blonde hair with a laugh. "Last time I saw him he was headed back to the little boy's room to vomit some more. So I split."

"You left the prom?"

She batted her large blue eyes at Lindy.

"Yes, I left the prom. I have my daddy's car. Come on. Let's go for a drive."

"I don't believe you. Why are you asking me to go?" She narrowed her eyes, suddenly suspicious.

"You wanna know the truth, Lindy?"

"Yeah."

"I know what you are. That's why I avoided you at school. I know because I'm one too."

"Get out of here. Are you drunk, Jeanne? Hey,

quit horsing around with me. This is a setup, right? Hal and some of the guys are probably waiting to jump me in the parking lot. You're going to drive me there and dump me. That's pathetic. Go on, Jeanne, leave me alone. It's not going to work. What do think I am, stupid?"

"Is that what you think?" Jeanne shook her head slowly from side to side. "All right, then" she added, in a small voice. "I'll leave."

"Wait," Lindy called. "What you said about being one too. You mean it?"

Jeanne nodded. "I think I've known since I was a little girl."

Lindy had gotten into the car. They went to a drive-in for Cokes, then parked and necked until dawn.

Helene was proud of herself. She had made her first standing rib roast. So what if she followed the recipe. That's what they were for. After the beef had cooled, she cut slices into thin strips. Slivered green and red peppers, scallions. Steamed the pea pods. Toasted sesame seeds in a cast iron skillet. Then she tossed everything together with olive oil, balsamic vinegar, and pepper, and placed the bowl in the refrigerator.

The kitchen was redolent with the smell of roast beef and sesame seeds. Helene brought her fingers up to her nose, where the myriad flavors of the food were also in evidence. She smiled and licked her fingers. The evening was just beginning.

Now she had to figure out what she was going to wear.

Lindy packed the chicken and potato salad into the wicker picnic basket along with a chilled bottle of nonalcoholic sparkling wine. She double-checked to see that she had taken everything she needed, set the basket on the kitchen table, and went upstairs to change.

When Helene knocked on the door of Room 1206, Lindy was waiting. The table was set for two. Candles were burning, and a tall vase of yellow roses stood at elegant attention.

"It's good to see you," Helene said.

Lindy embraced her and caught a whiff of her perfume along with a hint of sesame.

They kissed. Lindy took out Helene's bowl of salad and a sourdough baguette. Two pears rested at the bottom of the paper bag. Lindy placed everything on the table.

"I'm hungry." She uncovered Helene's salad. "Umm. Is this what I think it is? A beef salad? Great. There was a recipe for it in the food section a few weeks ago that I really wanted to try, but I threw away the newspaper before I remembered to cut it out."

"That's the one. Marinated beef salad. I guess my roommate had the same idea and cut it out. Good thing, no?" The smile lit up her whole face.

Lindy took her hand and drew her close. They kissed again, this time longer, with a violent passion that startled them both. As they broke away from one another, Helene bumped into the table.

"We'd better sit down on the couch before we upset something."

"Wait a minute, I thought you were hungry," Helene whispered.

"I am. But I've been meaning to find out since the day I read your ad what it is that you love to eat."

"Oh, have you now?"

"Yes, I have."

"Take off your shirt then."

Lindy did so.

"Loosen your belt and unzip your pants for me

real slow. That's right. Oh," she moaned, "oh my. I love a butch who knows how to take direction."

Helene moved closer, her high heels soundless on the carpet. She placed both hands on Lindy's breasts, bent her head and sucked on the nipples.

Lindy stifled a gasp. Her nipples were more sensitive than she remembered. Or perhaps it was the way Helene was sucking relentlessly. She felt sharp fingernails on her back, soft lips grazing her cheek, then covering her mouth. Teeth digging into her shoulder. Fingers grabbing at her ass. Hands pulling down her boxer shorts, caressing the hair that covered her pubis. A hard knuckle opening her labia, nudging against her clit. Fingers entering her.

Lindy cried out as expert hands moved her to orgasm.

"What strong legs you have," Helene murmured, stroking the length of Lindy's thighs. "I love butch women with strong, hairy legs. Stay right where you are, on your two feet. I'm not finished eating."

Helene took off her skirt, revealing stockings, a garter belt, and no panties. She got down on her knees and pulled Lindy to her.

"This is my favorite food. This is what I love to eat."

sweat

The down comforter ended up bunched on the floor. Lenox lay on top of me, the denimed cheeks of her firm ass in the palms of my hands.

"God, what a great ass you have."

"That's 'cause it's clothed."

I lifted my face from the tangle of her hair.

"Who taught you that? You're supposed to accept a compliment graciously, not toss it back."

"Right. Sorry."

"Give me another kiss then, and I'll forgive you."

"Sure. I'll gladly kiss you any time. Any where. Any place."

"Quit talking and give me your lips. Now, you brat," I laughed.

So she kissed me. The girl's got a great mouth and a tongue that knows its business. I moaned from deep inside. I didn't know I could make any sounds with a tongue like hers filling my mouth. But I did.

My hands moved from her ass cheeks to her thighs, then her crotch. She pushed against me and the hard-edged seams of her jeans dug into my flesh.

"You're warm down there," I said, pulling away to take in a breath.

"Umm," she replied, biting on my earlobe.

"Careful."

"Umm."

Her tongue thrust itself deep into the labyrinth of my ear in answer.

Shivers shook my body. I felt myself lifting, floating, etherized. A tongue in the ear can do that to me.

"Lenox, oh baby," I finally managed, trying to anchor myself to her before the sensation engulfed me completely.

Thankfully she moved to my neck, nibbling and tickling as her lips traveled down to one breast. I felt the sharp edges of her teeth teasing my nipple, which responded immediately, hardening.

"Umm," she murmured in satisfaction, then moved to attend to the other nipple. Soon it, too, stood erect. Lenox sighed and rubbed her wet face on my chest.

"You're soaked with sweat. No wonder. It's hot in here and you're still fully dressed. Come on, take off your clothes."

I lay her down and knelt over her. Sweat glistened on her skin.

I licked her neck. Ran my tongue down to her armpits and lapped at her salty hair. A sharp, spicy scent like cloves in hot cider rose from her wet skin. I moved to her breast. Under the ministrations of my tongue, her pectoral muscles seemed to swell, solidify. I alternately took each nipple in my mouth and sucked on them with a brutal energy. Low sounds emanated from her lips.

"What, Lenox? Talk to me, baby. Should I stop? Huh? Is that what you want?"

She shook her head wildly, as if begging for her life.

My hand reached between her legs. She was so wet. Oh, she was wet.

I pushed three fingers inside her, swiveling my hand so that my thumb rested on the hard nub of her clit. Then my arm came to life, and my whole body along with it.

Sweet, sweet wetness. It felt so fine to fuck her. She was wet with sweat, wet with juices, wet with come.

When her convulsions began, she tightened her legs around my waist and squeezed the breath from me.

I had met her only a week before. She had been wearing a short black skirt, and even in the dim light of the bar I could see the well-formed shape of her legs. I caught her looking at me a number of times, undisguised admiration in her eyes.

Later she brushed against me and said, "Crowded in here, isn't it?"

I nodded and smiled in agreement.

"You've got terrific legs," I said. "What do you do? Let me guess. You're either a dancer or a cyclist."

"You sound sure of yourself. But no," she replied, "I'm not either. You'll never guess."

"You teach aerobics then. Am I warm at least?"

"No, not a bit," she laughed. "I'm a waitress."

When I signed on, the familiar voice greeted me: "You've got mail."

Date: Sat, Jul 29, 1995 1:16 PM EDT. From: NoShyGrl. Subj: Wet. To: BtchTop. I hope you enjoyed yourself as much as I did last night. *How* did you manage to get that huge dildo inside me? Between your big cock and my bruised knees I can hardly walk. P.S. I'm still wet with my juices and your come.

Reply: Yes, yes, yes. I, too, enjoyed myself immensely. Girl, you sure have a mouth on you. And *what* a tongue. I read somewhere about smokers and their oral fixations. You can oral me anytime! ;-) And yes, we will be using *big* dildos to get you good and ready for my fist. I can't wait. Can you?

From: NoShyGrl. Subj: Re: big dildos. I can oral you anytime. How about now? Can I come over? P.S. When will I be ready for your fist? Soon, I hope. I'm getting wet just thinking about it.

Reply: Better get a lot of rest before our next date (Fri night!) so you won't be tired. I promise you it will be one *long* night.

From: NoShyGrl. Subj: Fri night. I will be well-rested, I promise. I am taking the day off and have no plans other than to be ready for you. There will be strawberries, grapes, and sparkling water in the fridge. I will be bathed and oiled and ready. P.S. I shaved myself *all over*. Yes, my pubes too, the way you fantasized. I'm smooth all over. P.P.S. Don't want to be too pushy, but can you take me through it now so I can anticipate it for the rest of the week? Imagine how wet I'll be by then. ;-)

Reply: The strands of leather caress your back. I flick my wrist in a circular motion. The strands sweep through the air and brush against your skin. Lightly at first, then harder and harder. The blows rain with full force on your muscled back. I kiss your hot skin, red now and glistening with sweat. I turn you over, lick your lips, kiss your mouth. I raise your thighs and position myself so that I am sitting in front of you with my thighs under your outstretched legs. I pull on a glove, reach for the lube. You watch as I squeeze the tube, your eyes shining. I enter you slowly with two fingers, then three. I place the butt of my other hand on your pubis, sliding it up and down your smooth mound until I find your clit in its hidden place. My fingers are fucking you slow and deep. You push your hips up to meet them, greedy to be filled. Are you ready for more? Are you ready for my fist? You moan, twisting your head from side to side. I spread more lube onto my hand, around the knuckles, insert my little finger, my thumb, squeezing my hand into a point. I push, push, deeper with each stroke. I rub your clit harder now, faster, eliciting low moans. I'm going to give it to you. I'm going to hurt you and fill you and you're going to beg me not to stop. I push in, feeling the resistance at the ring of my knuckles. Open up for me now. I'm going to take you, I'm coming in. I push against you. Your mouth opens in a scream and ends in a moan as my fist slides home.

That's all I'm going to say. I hope you get the picture.

From: NoShyGrl. Subj: Your fist. Yes, I've got the picture. You have my full attention. I'm as wet as the sea and about as deep. Come inside me and feel the fire.

Reply: I will.

Rain

Georgia lay in bed listening to the rhythm of the rain. It was a steady, comforting sound. Good thing she had finished in the garden. She had spent the last two days bent over, mulching and weeding, and her lower back was aching like nobody's business. She rubbed her hands together gingerly. Her right hand was stiff, the joints swollen and red. Arthritis had changed Georgia's hands into bunched alien appendages, a constant, nagging source of pain.

"Hands bothering you again?"

Georgia turned. Lou, her partner of thirty years, was sitting in bed, reading a paperback. A Kate Delafield mystery.

"Yes," she replied. "Fingers, hands, arms, back. You name the place, I hurt. I hurt everywhere. What is it about growing old? My whole body is giving out."

"Your body and mine both. I don't know, Georgie. Seems like just yesterday I was sixteen."

"Yes, and now we're both nearing eighty."

"Don't exaggerate. Sixty is not nearing eighty! But don't remind me."

Georgia sighed deeply, a sound like an expiration from a bellows.

"This hurts, that hurts, everything hurts. The question is not what hurts but what doesn't. My hands are singing the loudest. Shrieking some very high notes."

But Lou had already turned back to her book.

Georgia switched off her reading light and plumped up the feather pillow, arranging the other one in front of her, so she could lie on her side and spoon.

She closed her eyes against the light from Lou's side of the bed and yawned. She was dead tired, but her mind was racing. And her hands were screaming, You fool. Let someone else's fingers play in the earth and uproot weeds. You are too old. You think you're still sixteen? Hah! Those were the days when you could make love all night long, take a shower, grab a cup of coffee, and go to work, wet hair and all. Those were the days.

She had just turned sweet sixteen when Anne became her first lover. Besides Anne, she couldn't remember much from the year she was sixteen. There were so many lapses in her memory now.

But she certainly remembered the day she fell in love with Lou.

It was a Sunday afternoon and she was having a vodka gimlet at a lesbian bar on Cole. Georgia was in the habit of going to Maud's for a cocktail before returning home to prepare a leisurely Sunday dinner.

A woman entered the bar, rain falling from her, hair plastered to her head. She walked straight to the bathroom, draping her jacket on a bar stool as she passed.

"A regular I've never seen?" Georgia asked the bartender.

Ellie shrugged.

"Don't think so. She's not a familiar face to me."

"Must be a regular. She knows right where the loo is."

When the woman came out of the bathroom, she walked to the bar and ordered a draft beer.

"Heck of a day outside," Ellie said as she set down the drink.

"Yes. Everyone says we need the rain, it's been dry for so long. But I have a bike and I much prefer dry asphalt."

Georgia studied her from the relative safety of the shadows. She was hunched over her drink as if she were protecting it. Though she looked young, the woman's brown hair was flecked with gray. A pair of spectacles perched on the bridge of a sharp nose. Her hands were large, and a restless finger moved up and down the side of the glass. Georgia tried to imagine the woman's big hands on the handlebars of a Schwinn.

When Ellie moved to a customer at the other end of the bar, Georgia ventured over. "Hello, I'm Georgia. You new in town?"

The woman turned toward her.

"No, I was born in the city. I've just never been in here before."

"You were born here? No kidding. You're the first native San Franciscan I've ever met. It seems like everybody moves here from somewhere else. I was beginning to think no one's actually from here."

"I was born at Saint Luke's. Grew up on Potrero Hill."

"Cigarette?"

They both lit up. The woman started coughing and grinned sheepishly.

"Actually, I don't smoke. Oh, by the way, my name's Lou. Short for Louise."

"Hi, Lou."

A long silence followed.

"Yes, I've passed by here many times but," Lou shrugged, "new bars are always intimidating, no matter how dark the place is. I mean, where do you go? It's so hard to meet people."

Georgia smiled and nodded in agreement.

Lou drained her drink and stood.

"Better be off."

"What's the hurry? You just got here. Besides, the

longer you stay, the more people you're likely to meet. Come on, stay awhile," Georgia urged.

Lou looked around her. In the corner, two women shot pool. A couple sat around a table covered with drinks. One woman stood forlornly beside the juke-box. Mounted on the wall above the bar was a TV with the sound turned off. Georgia and Lou and another woman were the only ones at the bar. Marvin Gaye crooned, "Let's get it on."

"Well, it is a Sunday. But it's not usually this slow. It'll pick up, really. Come on. I'll buy the next round."

"Thanks, but I don't usually drink."

"Don't drink, don't smoke. What do you do?" Georgia laughed.

"I write," she said. "I'm a poet." There was a ring of pride in her voice.

It was the way she said it. I'm a poet. That's how Georgia fell in love.

The next Sunday Georgia had returned to Maud's in anxious anticipation. When Lou walked in, she felt an instant serenity. Lou had two beers but declined a cigarette.

The Sunday after that, Georgia bought a rib roast and placed it in the oven on low before she went to Maud's. In the refrigerator was a green salad and a Sara Lee pound cake. She set the table for two and uncorked a bottle of Napa burgundy to breathe.

Lou was not at the bar. An hour later, when she still had not showed, Georgia started to despair about her rib roast. It was a four-pound bone-in roast, and Georgia liked her meat rare. She calculated that if she did not go home to take it out of the oven in thirty minutes, it would be ruined.

She was getting ready to leave when Lou ran in, waving a notebook.

"Hi. Want to hear a poem?" Lou greeted her.

"Yes, I'd love to. But if I don't leave now, there'll be a disaster at my place."

"Why? What's the—"

"Look, I've got to run for the streetcar. Want to meet me at my house? Just bring your bike up to the apartment, okay?"

Lou grinned at her.

"I can't bring the bike up, but I'll take you home on it."

That was her first time on a motorcycle. And the roast was perfect.

The Sunday after that, Lou came for dinner and stayed. Georgia could still remember every detail like it was yesterday.

They had feasted on cracked crab from Fisherman's Wharf spread out on newspapers on the kitchen table. There was a loaf of sourdough and a handful of radishes, sweet reds and peppery whites from Georgia's garden. They shared a bottle of white wine and a bar of dark chocolate.

"My hands smell like chocolate and crab meat. Delightful delicacies, but I'm not sure it works as a combo," Lou had laughed.

"That's why I got extra lemons."

Georgia cut a lemon in half and rubbed the juice on her hands.

"That's how you get rid of the smell."

But Lou leaned toward her.

"I'm not sure I want to get rid of the smell. I like it. I like the taste, I like the smell. I like you."

She leaned in for the first kiss.

Remembering back, Georgia could have sworn the kiss went on for hours but, as unreliable as her memory had become, maybe it didn't last quite that long. Lou's arms locked around her. They felt astonishingly strong. Somehow their clothes were gone because

Georgia felt the uneven texture of the wool afghan from the bed on her skin. The next thing she recalled was Lou's hot breathing on her neck as they rocked together, straining toward their separate climaxes.

Georgia was startled to find that she was aroused. She was wet. She knew it even without touching herself. That in itself was wondrous. As she had gotten older, she had gotten less wet. She couldn't remember the last time they had made love. Couldn't remember at all. Had it been a month ago, or was it six? Surely they had made love at least once this year. But she couldn't recall.

When they were first together they could hardly get out of bed. In those years there were no demonstrations of affection like the young ones now who thought nothing of kissing and touching and parading about in public with half their clothes off. But once they were behind closed doors, they couldn't keep their hands off each other. They had frequently made love several times a day.

In time, of course, the frequency lessened. Weekly. Monthly. Birthdays, anniversaries, holidays. These days they read in companionable silence, kissed each other good night, and fell asleep spooning their pillows.

Georgia was feeling amorous tonight, though. Lou's reading light was still on, but when she turned toward her, she saw that the book had fallen shut and Lou was fast asleep.

A week later was their monthly trip north to visit an old friend who was recovering from radiation treatments. Eleanor lived alone in a cottage in Bodega Bay with her two English bulldogs, Sam Spade and Sarah Sweetheart. She was eighty years old and full of lively wit. A year ago, doctors had found cancer and set up an aggressive program of radiation and chemotherapy.

She had undergone radiation for six months but had adamantly refused to do chemotherapy.

"It's my body and I will not have chemo, that's all. That's it. End of discussion. I may be old, I may be plain, but it's my body. It's all I have."

The doctors had insisted on the chemotherapy, but she had stuck to her guns. Although the cancer was now in remission, the radiation had not been kind. Ulcers that refused to heal had erupted on both legs. Eleanor had been a fiercely independent woman who loved to walk. Now she was confined to her house and unable to function without a walker. Fortunately, she had her dogs, and her dogs had a large fenced-in yard that overlooked the bay.

Georgia and Lou visited every month, bringing new books and provisions from the city.

Since their trusty Volvo was in the shop for repairs, Daniel, their neighbor, had offered the use of his vehicle. Daniel was gay. They had been neighbors and good friends for ten years. He had recently bought a Bronco, and both women had admired his new acquisition.

They were grateful to him for his generous offer and had accepted at once. As they packed for their trip, they felt as excited as teenagers at the prospect of driving the new car.

As usual, Georgia picked vegetables from the garden at the last minute and stowed them carefully in a box. There was yellow squash, carrots, tomatoes, and green peppers. A bunch of chives, one of curly parsley, and handfuls of thyme, rosemary, sage, and comfrey leaves.

As usual, on their way, they stopped at Peroski's Poultry just outside Petaluma and bought two smoked chickens. Some forty minutes later, as they were approaching the ocean highway, it started to rain.

"Oh, look at that. It has to rain the last hour, wouldn't you know it. And just as we're getting to the winding coastal road."

"We could pull over at the next restaurant and wait it out."

"I'm not hungry. And I'd like to be there. Couldn't it have waited until we got there before it started?"

The rain fell harder as if in response.

"Well, I'm getting hungry. Why don't we stop in one of those rest areas overlooking the ocean and have a snack. We'll wait a little while, and then I'll drive the rest of the way, all right?"

"I suppose it won't hurt to stop."

"You need to eat something, Lou. You're getting snippy."

Georgia brought out the picnic basket. There was a sourdough loaf and a block of sharp cheddar. Lou unwrapped one of the smoked chickens and cut into the breast.

"Want a carrot?"

"Oh, my, these little carrots are sweet!"

They ate in silence while the rain drummed against the roof of the car.

"You know, I haven't smoked in five years and this is when I miss it the most."

"I can't imagine that at all. How can you foul your mouth with smoke when the flavors of the food are still fresh in it?" Lou asked.

Georgia fixed her with a look.

"I'm not criticizing you. I'm just saying I can't imagine it, that's all."

The windows had steamed up. Lou wiped her window with a paper napkin and looked out at the ocean.

Georgia finished a piece of chicken, licked her fingers, and sighed.

"Do you remember my three favorite smells?"

"Of course. The smell of garlic, the smell of wood smoke. And the smell of a woman." She looked at her lover. "What brought that up?"

"Nothing. The chicken, I suppose. The smell of the smoke on my fingers. You know, the other night I was thinking about the first time we made love. And I got aroused."

"Did it surprise you?"

"Well, yes, I...I haven't felt amorous for months."

"Do you feel bad about it?"

"No, we aren't young anymore. I expect our urges decrease, or something like that."

"You sound so clinical."

They both laughed. The rain pinged on the roof of the car like hail.

"It's really bad out there. How much further is it?"

"Not too far. Look and see if there's a map in the glove compartment."

Instead of a map, Georgia found condoms and a tube of something or other.

"Oh, look what Dennis keeps in his glove compartment. Those boys!"

"Well, at least he's prepared. What's that tube?"

"It's something called ForPlay Sensual Lubricant."

"Sensual lubricant? Maybe it's the stuff they use to make you wet when you're not? Let me see that. What do you think it feels like?"

"Let's open it and see."

They each squeezed a dab onto their fingers, giggling like teenagers.

"I wonder what it feels like down there," Georgia grinned wickedly.

"Want to try?" Lou whispered. She reached inside the waistband of Georgia's sweatpants and moved her hand to the warmth.

"Oh, it's cold!"

"Shall I stop?"

"Ohh, ohh," Georgia murmured as Lou's sure fingers stroked the gel onto her genitals.

Her lips opened as Lou's mouth pressed against hers. She could taste the smoky fragrance on her lover's tongue. Lou brushed against her breast and before she knew it, a groan escaped from her lips. She felt wetness down there, sweet wetness. The combination of the familiar sensation and the newness of it excited her. Lou was stroking her harder and harder. She had almost forgotten what it felt like. Oh, she wanted her, she wanted it, she wanted...she wanted to be filled.

She broke away from the kiss.

"What is it? Are you all right?"

Georgia nodded.

"I, I want—"

Then she saw it. The yellow squash in the box. She reached for it and held it in her hand. Lou stared at her, an incredulous look on her face. Georgia opened a pack of Trojans and pulled the condom over the squash with an expertise she did not know she had. Without a word then, Lou uncapped the lubricant, smeared a liberal amount onto her hand and rubbed it on the sheathed squash.

Georgia closed her eyes and lay back in the seat. The rain sounded sonorous, sweet as a Gregorian chant.

As Lou rocked her and stroked her, she could feel herself lift. She was flying, soaring through the clouds, the wind in her hair. She saw the Castro below her, teeming with youngsters in tight jeans and tank tops, baggy shorts and oversized shirts. Their muscles bulged. Their tanned skin, sheened with sweat, shone in the sunlight. They wore work boots and leather vests, Birkenstocks and Levis. They were tattooed. Pierced and proud. They sported labyris medallions and double women's symbols on chains around their necks. They kissed and hugged openly on the street.

She saw a young butch with short-cropped hair, torn jeans, and a faded denim shirt smiling up at her. Her teeth were white. Her eyes flashed a brilliant aquamarine. The woman's arm came up in a fist, a fast, deliberate upward motion. A salute of the clan.

"Yeeeess!" The young butch cheered at the top of her lungs.

Age, thought Georgia. What was that? She was free. She felt no pain in her hands. No ache in her back. There was joy in her heart and a song on her lips. She was crying, she was moaning.

Yeeeess!

And the rain fell like autumn leaves.

i go out walking

I stepped out of Kirsten's tent and put on my boots. The morning was alive with birdsong. I opened my arms to the new day, stretched and filled my lungs with its scent. The air was clean following the storm of the night before, and humidity had not yet taken over the day.

This was my first time at Michigan and my last day on the land. The experience had been, in a word, heaven—bugs, the heat, and the bland festival fare notwithstanding. I had played and partied all week long. On the land with a reported one hundred and fifty thousand women. Yes!

Now the festival was ending and I did not want to return to the real world. I'm not sure that any girl was ready to go back.

"Lover..." Kirsten's voice broke into my thoughts. "You forgot something."

An arm appeared from the tent holding aloft a dildo dangling from a leather harness.

"Oh, thanks." I beamed at her as memories of the night flooded into my mind. "I left a T-shirt, too. Can you hand it to me? I think I should cover this."

Kirsten poked her head out of the tent.

"Why, lover?" A wicked grin split her face. "It's such a lovely cock. And the things you do with it! I think you should just sling it over your shoulder."

"You're kidding, right? I've got to walk up the main street, go past RV parking, DART RV, and then the showers. Think of all the women I'll pass to get back to my campsite."

"I am, lover. I am."

And we both burst out laughing.

"If you do it, do it all the way," Kirsten said. "You should take off your shirt and show the marks on your back. I think they're beautiful myself."

A slow smile blossomed on my face.

What the hell, I thought, giddy as a rush of cockiness shot from my crotch and exploded in my head. Where else could I walk naked through the fields, with a dildo over my shoulder? Where else but at Michigan.

I took off my clothes and Kirsten folded them into a tidy bundle.

"Thanks."

"No, lover. Thank *you.* "She leaned back and looked up at me. "What a sight you are—a big tanned butch top wearing boots and carrying a cock over your shoulder. You are truly a vision."

So I went out walking like that.

Women stared, did double takes. Some smiled. Some turned away, embarrassment etched on their faces. Others nodded in approval and gave a thumbs up.

As I walked, I recalled the night.

Me underneath Kirsten as she rocked above me, my cock deep inside her. My hands clenching the muscles of her ass as she threw her head back and bellowed into the night sky at the point of her climax.

Later we lay in the grass in a pool of moonlight and kissed tenderly, lingering in the moment. My fingers in her hair, her tongue in my mouth.

Yes, I will recall with much pleasure the time I walked naked through the fields with my cock slung over my shoulder. I will remember it all the days of my life.

I will. Every time I go out walking.

unforgettable

Unforgettable.

It was the name of the song by Nat King Cole. It was also the word that Suz would later use to describe I.C., Isabel Ching according to the name on her driver's license. But I.C. would kill anyone who called her Isabel. And, or so the rumors went, almost had.

Suz had first seen I.C. at the Abbey, a coffeehouse on Massachusetts Avenue. She was eating a roast beef sandwich with caramelized onions on sourdough when she caught a whiff of smoke. Suz hated cigarette smoke, especially when she was eating. And she was sitting in the window area filled with wingback chairs, the No Smoking section. She looked around in annoyance.

A cloud of smoke rose from one of the wingbacks by the door. Suz pushed away her plate and got up.

"D'you know you're in the No Smoking section?"

Suz found herself staring at an impassive face. It looked vaguely Asian, but the short black hair was wavy. It was a serious face. *Inscrutable* was the first word that popped into her head.

"So?"

The woman was holding a newly lit cigar in a large hand. Suz found herself drawn to the hand like a magnet to a refrigerator door.

"Cat got your tongue?" the woman sneered. "I know I look like a foreigner but I do speak English."

"What? Oh, yes, of course, I...," she stammered. What the hell was wrong with her?

"You were saying?"

"I—"

"I assume you came over here to say something to me," the woman pressed. "What?"

"It's just that you're sitting in the No Smoking section and I didn't know if you knew."

"Yes, I do. Thank you, though. Anyway, there are no empty tables."

The woman took some puffs off her cigar and turned away. Suz had been dismissed.

She went back to her table and stared at her half-empty plate. The fragrance of the cigar smoke filled her senses. It was strangely pleasing.

The next evening Suz and her best friend, Leeza, went to the Abbey for coffee after the movies. Leeza was having girlfriend problems again and wanted to process.

As Suz was taking her first bite of raspberry torte, the door banged shut and she looked up to see the woman of the previous evening enter. She wore black Levis, boots, a gray shirt, and leather suspenders. Something caught in Suz's chest.

"Suz?" Leeza said. "You alright?"

"Uh, yeah," she breathed as the woman strode past their table without giving her a glance.

"What was that about? You should have seen the look on your face. You know the woman or something?"

"Not exactly, but I'd sure like to."

Suz went to the Abbey again the following night. The woman was there. She sat in a wingback chair sipping an iced drink.

Suz ordered a latte.

"Hi, Trixie," she greeted the woman at the counter.

"Hey, how's it going?"

"Great. You?"

"Eh, no complaints. Not yet, anyway," Trixie answered.

"Say, who's that woman over there? Do you know her?"

"Where?"

"Over there, in front of the windows. She looks kind of Asian or something."

"Oh, that's I.C. She's half Asian and half Mexican."

"I.C.?"

Trixie laughed. "Yeah, icy I.C., that's what they call her."

"Why?"

Trixie winked at her as she turned to the next customer.

"Guess you'll find out if you're interested enough."

Suz took the mug firmly in her hand and approached I.C.'s table.

"May I join you?"

The woman shrugged. "You can't harass me yet. I haven't started smoking."

"I'm Suz, and no, I'm not here to harass you."

The woman gestured to a chair. Her large hand caught the light.

"And I'm I.C., otherwise known as Icy."

Suz sat down and stirred her latte.

"Icy, huh? How did you get that nickname?"

"Well, here in the bar I'm known as Icy because I'm just the opposite. You know, fiery Mexican though mixed with stoic Chinese. But originally an evil ex gave me the name. It's a long story, and I sure don't want to go into it."

"Okay, I'm easy."

"How easy's that?"

"Are you flirting with me, I.C.?"

"Uh-huh. I like to flirt. It's a harmless activity, don't you think?"

"I suppose so. Me, I like the direct approach

method."

"What's that?"

"I'm really attracted to you and I'd like to take you to bed."

"Lots of girls would be turned off by that approach."

"Perhaps. But it works well for me."

"Good for you."

"So, how about it?"

"How about what?"

"What I said."

I.C. cracked a lopsided grin.

"You mean you weren't talking to a girl in a hypothetical situation?"

"No. I was talking to you."

"I like your approach. Suz, right?"

"Yes."

I.C. stood.

"Let's go."

damn safe sex

"Daddy:

"So here I am on my way home. Time has passed too quickly, much too quickly. I have savored every moment. Clung to each scene and every word that passed between us.

"I catch myself gasping for air as a remembered scene flashes before my eyes and I am left wanting. I think of our last kiss, how you pulled me into your mouth, pulled me to you by a fistful of hair. I melted.

"Daddy, Daddy, your boy melted like snow on a summer sidewalk, like the ice cream I spilled on your chest.

"Now that I am in the car speeding away from you, I hold on to my memories. I can feel my hands traveling down your stomach to your dark hair. I play on the outer edges of your lips, slowly spreading you apart. I take your nipple into my mouth, pulling it deeply in, feeling it harden against my tongue. I spread your lips open, then close them, all the while working your clit up and down. I want to drive you crazy with need. Your breathing begins to quicken as I tease you, giving attention to both nipples. I want you to beg for my boy-cock to pump you full.

"As I make my way down to your pussy, I cup your ass and pull you up to meet my hungry mouth. I begin to tongue and suck your lips. I breathe deep, taking in your scent. I am intoxicated. I can no longer curb my lust so I take you full in my mouth. I suck on your erect clit, savoring the taste of you. I bury my face in your cunt. My breathing becomes ragged, rough notes that tear the night. Instead of coming up for air, my mouth moves down to your crack. My tongue finds your sweet asshole and pushes in deep, deeper. My hands dig into your ass, squeezing, spreading, stroking...

"Daddy, I can't finish it. That's as far as I got. Please forgive any structural errors or typos. I just hung up the phone with you and am a little tired. I know you understand. It was great to come to the sound of your voice, but you know how I pass out afterwards. Perhaps you can find an ending to it. That would really be fun.

"See you soon.

Your boy robert"

"My sweet robert:

"Hello, baby boy. The days have been unbearable here, heavy with heat and high humidity. To add to that, I have had to work some very long hours. Yesterday I did get to come home before dark. I sat out on the back porch and watched the sky change as the sun set and a vast panorama of clouds patterned the sky. I saw nighthawks circling above me in the fading light, and I felt my heart lift and soar.

"It was good to get your letter. I must say, I got excited just reading it. You want Daddy to help you finish your letter? Is this going to be like the list? That first list I asked you to write when we were entering into our Daddy-boy relationship? I know you remember that. I wanted a list of ideal qualities in a boy, and I think out of the twelve that you wrote down, Daddy came up with half. Am I too lenient with you? Perhaps. But I do have a soft spot for my boy, and you know how to work it.

"This is different, I suppose, so let me sit down

with a fresh cup of coffee and see if I can put some words on paper.

"One of the advantages of being a Daddy is that Daddy knows everything. I know what you like and what you don't like. I know what makes you wet and what makes you cringe. I know how you like it and I know what makes you scream in anger or joy. Daddy knows.

"Remember the night you came to town for a holiday weekend and we went barhopping? We hit Paris, Berlin, and Visions before finishing the night at the Eagle. You were dressed in preppy boy drag, a royal blue shirt with a banded collar, jeans ironed with a sharp crease, and black boots. When we got to the Eagle I chatted with a friend. You walked ahead of me and started to go downstairs to the pit when the bouncer stopped you for a dress code violation. But that was before he saw your Daddy and realized that you were my boy.

"The bar was especially crowded that night. We stood cheek by jowl next to men with mustaches and chaps. Hatted and bare-chested. Drinking beer and smoking. No play occurred while we were there—the cross looking forlorn in the dim light, the restraints hanging like abandoned laundry.

"We had planned to meet some friends. They never showed up, though, so we left shortly after midnight. As we walked to the car you suddenly pulled me into a dark alley and pushed me up against a brick wall. I glanced at you sharply, but you merely flashed me a mischievous grin.

"'Daddy, I'm wet and hard and horny,' you said. 'Please, Sir, let me suck your cock and then fuck me, please. Fuck me, please. Please, Daddy, fuck me.'

"I looked around me but there were no signs of life. The neighborhood was asleep. 'Got a condom in your wallet like I taught you, boy?' Your face fell suddenly. 'No, Sir. I did carry one but I used it on you in the bathroom at Berlin. Sir, sorry, but I only had one. Let me give you a hand job, Sir, let me grip your cock in my fist. Let me feel the vein pulsing with blood, with life. Let me—'

"I slapped your face away. 'Shut up, boy. You're beginning to whine and you know damn well that gets on my nerves,' I said. I put a hand on your throat and pushed you away from me. 'Let's go home,' I growled. 'I'm going to put my fist in your cunt. I'm going to push my forearm up inside you.' You groaned and marched straight to the car without another word.

"Damn latex, I thought. Damn safe sex. What I wanted to do was hold you up against that brick wall and fuck your ass. I wanted to see the shaft disappear inside you as you screamed, Yes, Daddy. Yes.

"Now I can. I can do anything I want to do on paper, can't I? Damn safe sex, I'm going to fuck you in the ass without a condom. I'm going to put my fist in your cunt and tear you open, watch you bleed. Taste your blood. I'm going to rub my cunt in your open mouth. Have you tongue me, tongue me without the barrier of latex. Smell me, touch me, taste me. Fuck me."

"Daddy, you did it again. It happens every time. I'm hard, I'm wet, I'm horny. I'm hot for you. Please, will you allow me to do it to you just like that? Just one time? Please, Sir. I have no cuts or open sores. You know I'm sober and clean and healthy. Let me, Daddy, just one time. Let me taste you without a dental dam, without Saran Wrap. Let me suck you off without the taste of latex in my mouth. Let me fist you without a glove hampering my hand. Let me suck your cock without a sheath. Let me feel you flesh to flesh. Please, Daddy, please."

"boy:

"You know the answer. Yes, you can. In the next letter. As many times as you want. In ink. On paper. As for flesh to flesh in real life, boy, you damn well better know the answer to that."

seeking training partner

Somebody was in the shower. I could hear water hitting the tiles. I shut my locker, grabbed a clean towel, and padded toward the communal shower room.

Steam enveloped me as I entered, so much steam that I couldn't see. I breathed in, filling my lungs with its hot moisture. It was like walking into a wet sauna. I took another deep breath and the heat seared my lungs. I groped around for the wall so I could find the faucet and caught the sharp scent of wintergreen.

All of a sudden a pair of hands grabbed me by the waist and pulled me from my path.

"Hey, what's the—"

"Steady," said a voice. "I dropped my bar of soap and you were about to step on it."

I looked down at the floor. It was white with steam. I couldn't even see my feet, never mind a bar of soap. A pale body next to me bent over to pick something up. I could recognize the outline of her hips.

"There we go. Sorry, I didn't want you to have an accident."

"It's okay."

I saw the glint of the faucet set in the wall and reached to turn it on. The hot water pounded on my back like the hands of a masseuse, strong and sure.

I'm a bodybuilder, but I've been out of training for almost six months. After one particularly intense workout I left the gym to meet my lover for lunch and stepped off the curb into a storm drain. Even now, months later, I can hear the loud crack and feel the pain as it exploded in my foot. I fell into the street, clutching at my leg, and watched as my ankle swelled to the size of a grapefruit.

I had torn the ligaments in my right ankle. I spent three months on crutches, going to physical therapy twice a week. When I still could not walk, my doctor decided that the injury was more severe than he had first thought. He put me in a walking cast for three weeks. When that was taken off, my leg looked like it belonged to a stick figure, not a bodybuilder. I was mortified.

What I've done for the past few weeks is stretched, swam, and been bored out of my mind. My doctor told me to quit lifting, so I did. But I've got to get back into it again or I'll go nuts. Of course I promised him I'll be careful, avoid heavy leg workouts, but I'm determined to get back to the weights.

My training partner, a woman I had met at a state-wide meet, had recently married her girlfriend and moved out of town. So I decided to place an ad in a local gay paper to see if I could find another. I figured that having a partner would motivate me to get back on the program.

> Seeking Training Partner for
> morning workouts. Can travel.
> Your gym or mine. No novices.
> Sense of humor required.

No, sounds too much like an ad you'd find in the personals.

> Seeking Training Partner. Re-
> covering from an injury. Mainly
> free weights. Some powerlifting.
> Intermediate to advanced only.
> Serious-minded women espe-
> cially welcome.

Too intense.

I sat looking at the two ads until the words swam around in circles. So I merged them together.

> Seeking Training Partner for morning workouts. Recovering from an injury. Mainly free weights. Some powerlifting. Can travel. Your gym or mine. No novices. Sense of humor and serious-minded women especially welcome.

The ad had been in the paper for two weeks and I'd only gotten one response. A novice who was looking for a trainer. Don't people read?

I spent twenty minutes stretching, then warmed up on the Stairmaster. It was a beautiful day outside, and the gym was practically empty. I pulled on my workout gloves and walked to the leg press. I was determined to start with my weakest body part, so it was going to be a quad, hamstring, calf day. I started slowly, light weights, high reps. Short rest periods. Then to the leg extension machine, hamstring machine, seated and lying down. I counted out each rep, breathed deep, and exhaled with each exertion, willing my atrophied muscle fibers to fill with energy.

After forty minutes I could feel my muscles quivering. It made me feel good, like I had done some work for a change. My head felt light and I was shaking. Enough, I thought. Time to shower and get a bite to eat. Anyway, the gym was beginning to fill up.

As I came out of the locker room and walked through the free-weight area, I saw a woman stretching by the squat rack. Her head was down and both arms were pulling on the rack, stretching her lats and her arms. I saw the lines of her deltoids, triceps, and fore-arms. I smiled to myself as I passed her. I've always thought muscles were very sexy.

"Hey," called a voice.

I turned.

It was the woman at the squat rack. She was smil-ing at me.

"Hey, yourself," I said, smiling back at her. She definitely looked like a bodybuilder.

"I'm the one who saved the bar of soap from death and destruction at your feet."

"Oh, hi. June," I laughed, walking toward her, my hand extended.

"Hi, June, I'm Kim. I'm new here."

"Hey then, welcome to the gym."

"Thanks."

"I see you're just beginning your workout."

"Yeah, I tried to get in earlier but I had a fight with my partner."

She contorted her face in a grimace.

"Who do you train with?"

"No, not that. No one, at the moment. I meant, my lover."

"Oh. Sorry to hear that."

"It's nothing. We've been breaking up for weeks now, and it's just real hard."

"Yeah. Well..." I didn't know what else to say to her.

"It's okay," she said, reading my mind, "you don't have to say anything. Don't have to say anything at all. It happens."

"Yeah, I guess. I don't mean to sound trite or anything, but usually it works out for the best, though I know it probably doesn't feel like that right now."

"Yeah, I'm hurting and I feel pretty raw."

"Well, if you ever want to talk or work out together or something, I'm here most mornings. Or if you want to go have coffee sometime."

"Great. I'll keep that in mind."

"Yeah. See you around."

That night I had a dream.

I am at the gym and it is deserted. It is a warm, humid night and I am naked except for my workout gloves and leather sneakers. Lifting straps dangle from both wrists.

I spot a naked figure at the far end of the gym doing chin-ups at the chinning bar. As she lowers herself, her lats flare like wings, and as she pulls herself to the top of the position, her traps and delts stand out in bold relief. As I get closer, I see that it is Kim.

"Hey, where's your partner?" I call, then realize that she has no training partner. That her partner is her lover and they are breaking up.

But the figure does not heed me. She is whispering something. I approach, straining to hear. She is counting reps. Seventy-five. Seventy-six. Seventy-seven.

She's done seventy-seven chin-ups. I think, Jesus H. Christ!

"You okay?" I ask, "Kim, hey, you okay? What's going on?"

She continues to do chin-ups, counting each one out loud, determined, and not in the least bit breathless.

I look at this mechanical being in awe. Her muscles are pumped with blood and pulsing with power, sweat dripping from her body. Is this steely form real, or am I dreaming?

Just as I reach out to touch her, she falls, soundlessly crumpling to the floor at my feet.

"Kim, Kim!" I say in concern.

She raises her head at the sound of my voice.

"Oh, June, is that you?"

Her face seems to fold in on itself, her eyes squeeze shut. I see tears rolling down her cheeks as huge spasms shake her chest.

"Kim, I—"

"Just hold me," she sobs. "Please."

So I hold her in my arms as she cries, wailing as if her heart had been wrenched from her body.

"She lied to me. She said she needed to be alone, but I caught her with another woman. She...they were...they were fucking." The words fall from her lips, heavy as stones sinking to the bottom of a pond.

"God, I'm so sorry, so sorry." I have no other words.

I rock her in my arms, the weight of her comforting.

Then her hands begin to grope me. To my surprise, I feel her caressing my back. Her fingers move to my breasts. The roughness of the calluses on her hands excites me.

"Kim, what are you doing? I know you're upset, but I—"

She raises her head to the level of mine and before I know what is happening, she is kissing me hard, her tongue snaking into my mouth. When I pull away she says, "I need this, please. I want you to fuck me hard. Please, I need this release really badly."

Barely had the words left her lips than I cover her with my mouth. I draw her tongue as far inside me as I can. My hands devour her body, marveling at her mass, her muscles. Finally, I push her to the floor, spread her legs wide. I can smell her desire pulling me in. I touch her pubis shyly, her hairs tickling my fingertips. I open her petals, the scent of her now strong, enticing. She is so wet I plunge two fingers inside her, then three, thrusting until I can hear her ragged voice bursting in my ear. "Oh, yes, yes. Touch my clit now. I want to come. I need to come so badly. Oh, yes, please, now, yes."

With my other hand I find her clit, swollen, hard as a pearl, and I rub her in a rhythm as steady as the beating of my own heart. She comes in a frenzy, body jerking, eyes closed, shouting something I can't comprehend.

Afterwards, as I lie on top of her, she pushes her fingers deep inside me and I rock and thrust my hips into her, seeking my own climax.

"Oh, Kim," I cry out as I come.

The next day I got to the gym early, hoping that Kim was there. I did a light workout, then biked for forty-five minutes. Then I went twenty minutes longer. Still no Kim. I took a long shower, the room steaming as if water had been splashed onto hot rocks in a sauna.

I dressed slowly, reluctant to leave.

"Hey," a voice called out just as I exited the locker room.

"Kim! Say, are you okay?"

"Sure, why do you ask?"

"Oh, no reason in particular. It's just that...well, I was thinking about you, that's all. You know, you said you were going through a hard time and stuff."

"Oh, that. Hey, thanks for being concerned, but we're working it out."

"What?"

"My lover and I, we're going to make an effort to work it out. Problems, you know, everyone's got difficulties. We decided to not throw it all away without trying."

"Oh," I mumbled.

"Hey, three and a half years is nothing to sneeze at."

No, I thought, three and a half years is nothing to sneeze at. Hope my girl and I make it that long.

"No, of course not. Great. I'm glad for you."

"Yeah, me too. Hey, you okay? You look a little pale."

"No, I'm fine."

"Well, gotta get back to the weights. See you around." She beamed at me. It was a smile that said, I got laid last night and it was great.

"Yeah, sure." I shrugged and turned to leave. What else was there to say?

"Hey, June, you wanna work out together sometime?"

I looked at her tight, muscled body in her spandex suit and her big smile, and something inside me surrendered.

"Yeah," I nodded. "Sure. Sometime."

a Kodak moment

boy matt zipped himself carefully into his chaps, adjusted his harness for what seemed like the fifth time, and took a deep breath. Tonight was the night, and he wasn't sure he was ready. Tonight was the night that Mistress Lea was going down.

Earle surveyed the area with satisfaction. She had chosen a good spot. Moonlight flooded the meadow and bathed the tree in a white light. boy alexander had laid out the contents of the toy bag on a clean tarp and ringed the area with chairs. They were expecting a crowd.

Lea applied her lipstick with a practiced hand. When that was done, she realized she was shaking. What did she tell boy matt when he was nervous before a scene? "Breathe deep." Shit. It sure wasn't working for her.

boy alexander brewed coffee and checked the cooler again to make sure the soft drinks were chilling. This was his first time at the music festival in Michigan, and he wasn't at all sure that he liked doing the camping thing. His friends laughed and called him a prissy fag boy, but that didn't bother him. No, not at all. He liked his nails clean and manicured. He liked his white socks doubled-bleached so that they always looked brand new. And he liked his jeans ironed and his black curls combed and perfectly in place. A boy had to look good at all times, and the novelty of camping out was rapidly wearing thin.

Earle brushed her teeth and gargled. boy alexander

had been busy with preparations for the scene so she had dressed herself in the moonlight outside the tent. Now all she needed was for him to lace up her snakeskin gauntlets and she would be ready. She stretched and took a deep breath. Yes, she would be ready for Mistress Lea.

When Lea and boy matt approached, a silence descended on the crowd. Earle turned to greet them. Lea wore a leather gladiator bra and skimpy leather shorts. boy matt carried the toy bag. He was collared. It was time to begin.

"Please, Sir, may I kiss your hand," Lea said, dropping to her knees in front of Earle.

"Yes. You know this is how all my scenes begin. Kiss my hand," she ordered. "Kiss the hand that will beat you."

Lea kissed both hands, the fingers and each fingertip reverently. Then she raised her face to Earle.

"Tie her up to the tree, alexander," Earle instructed.

"Yes, Sir," came the reply.

Lea shivered when the first strokes started raining down on her back. It had been a long time since she had bottomed. She had spent the whole day anticipating the night, and now that it was here she was frightened.

The heavy leather flogger came alive in Earle's expert hands. The strands stroked, caressed, and stung Lea's skin. She bucked and shouted, "Daddy, oh Daddy. Ooohh."

Then the leather flogger was exchanged for a latex one, thin strands, sharp and stinging. Soon it was switched for another. One with broad, flat strands and a heavy, deep thud.

"Ooohh, Daddy," was all she could say. "Ooohh, Daddy."

The whip was an extension of her arm. Earle felt

its power as she wielded it in a circular motion, left side, right side, sweeping across Lea's skin like wind.

"'Oh, Daddy.' Is that all you can say? I'm going harder now, baby girl," Earle said. "This here is child's play and I'm getting bored. Wouldn't want you falling asleep on me. I'm going to take you further than you've ever been."

Lea nodded her head.

"What? You'd better speak if you're able to, girl. A nod will not do. What do you say, baby girl?"

"Please, Sir," she whispered, "yes, take me. Take me as far as you want. Take me as far as I can go."

"Good, baby girl. That's what Daddy wants to hear. matt, up off your knees and get over here. You've got work to do."

Earle arranged matt between Lea and the tree.

"Hold your mistress, boy. She's got my blood boiling and I'm going to beat the shit out of her."

When Earle approached the tree with a cat-o'-nine-tails, matt recoiled.

"boy," Earle shouted in his ear, "you're supposed to be holding your mistress while she's being beaten. You're supposed to be supporting her and taking care of her, not transferring your fear to her. alexander, get me the blindfold."

When Earle started up again, Lea screamed with each stroke and pulled herself up by her restraints, seeking to escape from the blows.

"Watch it, baby girl. You'll break my restraints. They're the second pair I've had to buy this year. Scream, baby girl, and stomp your feet. You will not break the tree or my restraints."

Five floggers later Earle was covered in sweat.

"Bring the water, alexander."

After Earle drank her fill, she took the bottle to boy matt.

"Take some for your mistress."

matt filled his mouth with water and offered it to his mistress.

"How are you doing, baby girl? Is it getting too much?"

"No, Sir, I want more, Sir. But can I have a kiss too?"

"No. You'll have to take a lot more to earn a kiss from me. But boy matt can give you one. Go ahead, boy. Give your mistress a kiss."

Earle moved to the tarp and surveyed the assortment of whips, canes, and crops.

"I have something you may wish to try," came a voice from the front row.

Earle looked up. A handsome butch with short-cropped blonde hair stood to attention. She wore a black shirt with a leather vest, a pair of perfectly ironed black jeans, and spit-shined engineer boots. At her waist was a heavy studded belt.

"Loren," she said, extending her hand.

"A pleasure, I'm sure," Earle returned.

"This is my favorite belt. The end of it has a sharp bite, and if you use it folded in half with the studs out, it leaves big old nasty bruises."

Earle smiled as the woman removed her belt.

"Thank you. I will try it."

Earle wrapped the belt around her fist, slapped the end on her open palm. She nodded with satisfaction.

"I'm going to give your back a rest, baby girl. Loren has graciously offered her belt, and I'm going to work your ass over with it. Think you can take that?"

"Yes, Sir," Lea whispered. "I'll try."

Earle began with quick slapping motions on Lea's ass cheeks.

"How does that feel? Good? Too light? Well, let's

go harder then, shall we?"

She hit the right cheek, then followed quickly with a backhand stroke on the left cheek. Lea screamed. matt flinched, as if he, too, had been struck.

"Ah, yes," Earle said. "Did you like that, baby girl?"

Lea nodded her head.

"I told you before a nod will not do. Tell the audience here."

"Yes, Sir," Lea whispered.

"Louder, I can't hear you. And if I can't hear you how will they? Louder," Earle bellowed.

"I like it, Sir. I like the belt."

"Good. Because I like it, too. I'm going to beat your ass silly. I'm going to make you earn your kiss. Water?"

alexander walked over immediately with the bottle in his hand.

Earle folded the belt in two and swung it. When it connected with Lea's flesh, she hollered, "God fucking damn!"

"God doesn't have a fucking damn thing to do with this. Do you like this? If so, thank me. If not, ask me to stop."

"Thank you, Sir, I like it. Oh, I like it."

Earle swung again. To the left, then to the right. Again. Again. And again.

"Thank you, Sir, oh, thank you, Sir," she sobbed.

boy matt stood shaking, his knuckles white where he was holding on to his mistress.

Lea's ass cheeks turned red and blue in the moonlight.

Earle gave the belt to alexander to hold. She put her hands on Lea's hot ass cheeks and kissed the nape of her neck.

"You did good, baby girl. And your back and ass look so fine. What reward do you want from Daddy?"

"I want my kiss, Daddy."

When Earle released Lea from the restraints, she fell into boy matt's arms. Earle gathered Lea up into her, bent her head back, and kissed her.

"boy matt, get your dick and put a condom on it."

"Yes, Sir."

"No, wait. Get your cock and have alexander put a condom on."

"Yes, Sir," the two boys replied in unison.

matt ran to the toy bag. He struggled with the dildo, trying to force it into the ring of the harness. alexander knelt patiently at his feet. Earle looked over in irritation.

"matt, for God's sake, take your time. Remember, when you are in my scene you are always on show. Put that cock on with some dignity, boy. I thought you were better trained than that."

"Yes, Sir. Sorry, Sir."

Earle turned Lea around, held her tight in her arms.

"Watch our boys, Lea. They're going to put on a show for us. boy alexander, you've been wanting to suck Daddy's cock, haven't you?"

"Yes, Sir. I've been waiting all day, Sir."

"Start with a boy cock then. Suck matt off, but don't either of you boys come without permission. Hear?"

"Yes, Sir."

When alexander took matt's cock in his mouth, Lea moaned.

"You want your Daddy's cock don't you, little girl?"

"Oh, yes, Daddy, yes."

"Does watching our boys get you wet?"

"Yes, but I've been wet, Sir. I started getting wet

when you were beating me."

"Is that right? I'll have to check you myself. On second thought, I think you should thank Loren for the use of her belt. What do you say?"

"Oh yes, Sir. Thank you, Loren," she murmured.

"No, baby girl, I think Loren should be thanked properly. Loren, get a glove and some lube and come over here, will you."

"Certainly."

"Will you help me check my baby girl. She says she's wet. We have to make sure she's wet enough to take a big cock."

Loren reached down to the tangle of hair. She sucked in her breath.

"Oh, yes, this little girl's very wet, Earle. Should I lube her up some more?"

"Please do. And give her throbbing cunt a good fucking with your hand, while you're at it, will you? I've got to put a condom on."

"Sir," called a voice from the audience.

Earle turned.

"Yes?"

"Sir, may I have the honor?"

Earle smiled.

"Of course. Come here."

A woman with long dark curls falling on her bare shoulders stood. She wore pink Saran Wrap around her breasts and loins. A triangle of dark hair peeked out from between her legs. She walked toward Earle, a look of defiance in her eyes. Her stiletto heels sank into the soil with each step, but she walked with a proud stride.

"And you are?" Earle smiled.

"Edwina, Sir."

"You look just wonderful, Edwina. Good enough to eat."

Earle spun her around.

"And you walked up here to the Twilight Zone dressed like this?"

"Yes, Sir. I wanted to look good for you, Sir."

"Ah, what a brave girl you are, Edwina."

"Sir, I would be most honored to put on your condom."

She dropped to her knees and rolled a condom on to Earle's cock with her mouth, in one smooth motion.

"Thank you, my dear. It looks like you're very adept at that."

"Thank you, Sir. I am skilled at many things, Sir."

"Are you now? Why don't you come to my tent later and show me your skills, Edwina."

"I would be glad to do that, Sir. Thank you."

Earle returned to Lea with a grin on her face. With all the energy and the attention at the camp, it was hard not to be full of herself.

"How's my girl doing, Loren?"

"Giving my hand a workout."

Earle grabbed a handful of Lea's hair and pulled her head to her.

"Want to suck cock, baby girl? Want Daddy's cock in your mouth?"

"Oh yes, Sir."

Earle held his stiff cock out while Loren bent Lea toward it. She took the head and half the shaft in one quick motion, then worked her mouth eagerly, her head bobbing back and forth, spittle spewing from her lips.

Earle beckoned to matt. Lea gasped when matt pushed his cock into her from behind and began pumping.

"alexander, get a dental dam, would you? And you know what to do with it?"

"Yes, Sir."

alexander got down on his knees behind Earle. He pushed apart her ass cheeks, spread the dental dam, and got to work.

"Nobody come without permission. Understood?"

"Yes, Sir," the group chorused.

In the meadow flooded with moonlight, the tree stood majestic, rising above the crowd gathered in the mist.

Loren took off her glove with a snap. She stood back, folded her arms across her chest, and surveyed the scene in front of her, a smile as bright as the moon on her face.

"What a splendid sight, yes indeed," she sighed. "This is definitely a Kodak moment."

Daddy and her girl

I called her Daddy on occasion. What occasion? Certain occasions that were alternately slow and sensuous or heated and charged with sexual tension. I called her Daddy when she had me spread out on the bed, limbs taut, and moved her lips and tongue all over me. Or when she caressed my back with the soft leather tails of her flogger.

I moaned for my Daddy when, in the darkness, I sensed the movement of her hands as she slipped on a glove and heard the sound of lube on latex. I moaned in the darkness because I could tell by how much lube she applied whether she was going to penetrate me with her fingers or with her whole fist. Just the thought of that fist inside me made me want to call her whatever she wanted.

We met by chance. At a marketing and promotions seminar for small businesses. I remember my first glimpse of her. I kept looking. She wore a black-and-white pin-striped suit, dark-seamed stockings with perfectly straight seams, and a pair of burgundy heels. Her black hair, perfectly styled, remained that way even after she had taken off her hat. She was a particularly striking woman who I guessed was in her late forties. She was definitely an older woman, and I've got this thing about older women.

I don't remember much from the seminar but I do remember the way she approached me. "I've had the *most* disagreeable week," she said to me by the croissants and coffee urn. "Looks like you have too, judging from the scowl on your face."

"Sorry," I replied hastily, "it's just a look of concentration, not displeasure."

"Glad you're getting something out of this," she continued. "I came hoping to learn some new strategies, but frankly it sounds like the same old things I heard when I first started my own business. Damned depressing. Hasn't anyone got any new ideas? What are we—damned dumb or what?"

I can't recall much about my side of the conversation. I guess I couldn't have been too inarticulate because she asked to exchange business cards. We did and I got a call from her not long after.

"Cameron Wells here," she said. "We met at the coffee urn last weekend."

I laughed, recognizing her voice on the other end of the line. What began as a routine call regarding computer systems, my specialty, ended with the scheduling of a dinner date.

We met a week later. She was dressed in a charcoal gray pantsuit and a teal blue silk blouse. She wore a black fedora on her head and high-heeled black boots. After the salmon mousse and shiitake mushroom appetizer, she propositioned me.

We've been meeting ever since. Once a week at the Langtry Inn, a bed and breakfast on Steiner Street by Alamo Park in the City. Every Thursday. We're both married. To women, of course. On Thursday afternoons her lover chairs a weekly sales and marketing meeting and mine goes to therapy. Cameron Wells and I have been seeing each other every Thursday for five months.

We have an arrangement that goes like this. I arrive at the hotel before noon on Thursdays dressed in blue jeans, T-shirt, cowboy boots and a black leather jacket. I carry a bag that contains certain items of erotic paraphernalia. Cameron arrives soon after with a picnic basket full of edibles and drinks.

She changes from whatever outfit she happens to be wearing to a tight-fitting jumpsuit made of glove-soft leather. Black leather. With a zipper that runs all the way from the low-cut top down to the crotch and through to the back of the ass.

The scene begins when Cameron enters the room. I relieve her of the groceries and whatever else she has in her hands. Then we kiss. She's got the most incredible lips. Soft, full, and usually painted some shade of red. I help her change into her jumpsuit. And spit-shined black boots. Then I hand her her favorite implement, an English riding crop.

She likes to sit in the armchair next to the bed and watch me take off my clothes. I always start with my boots and socks. Then I strip off my shirt, remove my heavy black belt, and take off my jeans. I stand in front of her, naked except for a pair of black lace panties. Sheer lace, or lace and silk or satin. She insists on black. No other colors or two-tones of any combination will do.

I'm not wearing much to begin with, but I strip slowly because I know she likes it when I put on a show for her. She sits in the armchair by the bed and plays with her riding crop, hitting the open palm of her left hand with deliberate strokes. Her eyes do not leave me for one second.

She has removed all her makeup. Her carefully coifed hair is slicked down and frames her head like a form-fitting helmet. Her face looks very hard and menacing. But I can tell by her eyes that she is looking at my body with great pleasure though no smile or other acknowledgment lights up her face.

Cameron Wells likes to play games of fantasy. When we first began our affair she told me she liked to play games.

"Sorry to disappoint you," I said, "but I'm not into cards, or board games either for that matter."

She laughed heartily and replied, "I like a woman who can make me laugh almost as much as I like multiple orgasms. Not those kinds of games, silly. I mean games of challenge, creativity, discipline, and daring. Are you up for it?"

What's a girl to say to a dare? I said yes.

"Good," she said, "this is your first lesson. Call me Daddy when we are in this room together. And obey everything I say."

"Yes, Daddy," I said, with some hesitation. Cameron, Daddy. Daddy? The words sounded strange coming from my mouth. What had I gotten myself into?

Cameron likes to use her hands. She likes to touch me all over my body. She likes to explore the ridges of my back, the curve of my biceps, the crack of my ass, my swollen clitoris and the bridge of my nose. Cameron also likes to use her riding crop, my leather belt and her many whips on my body.

I remember vividly the first time she whipped me. I was taking off my clothes when she commanded me to give her my belt. I did as I was told.

"Take off your panties too," she said. "I've been thinking about using a belt on your ass. Think you can take it?"

"Yes, Daddy." I answered as I'd been instructed.

"Get down on your knees and bend over the foot of the bed."

I did as I was told. I heard the sound of the buckle as she picked up my studded belt and wrapped it purposefully around her right hand. I heard the sound of leather as she brought it down on her open palm, testing the leather against her bare flesh. I felt myself holding my breath. I was mesmerized.

Then, before I could expel the breath, I felt the bite of leather on my bare ass. Again and again and again. Years of living as a tough dyke had taught me not to cry out. But I could not help myself. The impact of the belt shocked me with each blow. I heard myself and then, with great surprise, felt heat and wetness welling up between my legs.

Tears stung my eyes, my breath came in sharp gasps. After some time I felt Cameron down on the floor beside me. She put her mouth on the burning skin of my ass.

"How do you feel? Your ass is beautifully pink and *very* warm," she purred.

"I hurt like hell," I blurted. Then, remembering, I added, "I hurt like hell, Daddy. But I think I like it."

"Good girl. I know it hurts, but doesn't it hurt good? Don't answer," she said sharply, "I'll find out for myself."

She pushed my legs roughly apart. In the next instant I felt her fingers thrusting up inside me.

"It must hurt good, girl. You're dripping wet."

She turned me around to face her and kissed me hard. She pushed me down onto the floor and pressed her body on top of me. She took my nipple into her mouth and alternately sucked and flicked her tongue forcefully across the hardening tip.

My body was alive, wired with anticipation, and I shuddered when I heard the sharp snap of a latex glove. I moaned when she slid her fist inside me and my cries erupted when orgasms burst uncontrollably from within.

She held me in her arms until I stopped shaking, wrapped the strands of her softest flogger around my neck and whispered, "Baby, let me work on you all over again."

My lips and my eyes smiled. Yes, Daddy, yes.

one for all

I emerge from the shower and step into a darkened room.

As the room bursts into light, I see the tuxedo shirt hanging from the chandelier. It is a black shirt with silver pinstripes, a white collar, and French cuffs. Smart fucking aleck, I think, as I stand on a chair to retrieve it, the damp soles of my feet staining the upholstery. At least the shirt is perfectly ironed. And I see my black jade cuff links and studs in their place on the oak valet along with my motorcycle jacket. On the bed lies a pair of leather pants, a leather cummerbund, and my snakeskin bow tie. A yellow bandanna is neatly folded next to my boxer shorts. So, that's what she wants, is it? I'll make sure she gets it later. Damn right.

I've got a veritable circus planned for tonight, and I'll make my little girl moan, beg, bleed, scream, wet her pants, and come a dozen times before I'll let her kiss me. I save my kisses. I don't give them away for free.

I look for the toy bag and see it standing ready by the door. Good girl. She knows how to pack.

First things first. Before I get dressed it's my turn to pack. I pad across the floor in my bare feet and slide open the top drawer on the bedside table. I know dykes who name their dildos. Big Boy. Monster. Junior. Magnum. Glad Hand. Me, I know each of them by their length and their weight in my hand. Believe me, you won't find me calling my dick Li'l Bit. No way. Not any of them.

I dress slowly, folding back the cuffs, threading the studs into the buttonholes. Tuck the shirttails carefully into my pants, smoothing the fabric over the ten-inch cock that bulges proudly down one thigh.

I stand five feet six inches in my bare feet, but you wouldn't know it when I walk into a room dressed in leather. You wouldn't think it for a second. Not one second. Speaking of bare feet, where are my boots? And why have no socks been laid out for me? I'll cuff that girl yet. I go to my sock drawer and discover to my astonishment that it is empty. Damn. What is the girl playing at? I look at my watch. It's getting late and I'm beginning to get irritated.

At that moment the door buzzer sounds. Damn, I hate company before I'm ready. The buzzer shrills again.

I look through the peephole and see a cop, his peaked cap obscuring his eyes.

I fasten the chain and open the door a crack.

"Yes, officer?"

"Emergency on Elm Street," he says. "You ready? Let's go."

"Shit, no. She's hidden my socks."

"What? That's a new one." The cop starts to laugh.

"Shut up, Lem, and get in here," I say, closing and reopening the door.

Fifteen minutes later, Lem and I have ransacked the whole apartment and have not found a single sock. Even the dirty-laundry basket yields nothing. I am furious as I pull on my boots over bare feet. Bitch, I think, I'm going to get you good.

"When I get a hold of her I'm going to put your nightstick up her ass."

"Something we all know she loves," Lem snickers.

"Shut up, smart mouth," I snap, "or you won't be getting anything up yours."

That silences him right away, as I knew it would.

When we approach the house on Elm Street, there are no lights on inside. Our boots sound loudly on the paved footpath.

Lem raps his nightstick against the door.

"Anyone home? Open up. Police."

A breeze stirs the bamboo wind chimes that hang on the sun porch.

"Open up. This is your last chance." Lem tries again.

The sound of glass breaking shatters the silence. Somewhere on the block a dog barks.

"Quick," I snap, as Lem reaches through the broken pane and unlocks the door.

We walk down the dark hallway. To our left, the living room is filled with moonlight.

"Upstairs bedroom or to the kitchen?" Lem mouths.

I point to the end of the hallway.

The swinging wooden door is closed.

"You first," I instruct.

Lem pushes the door open with his nightstick, and we enter together. At that instant the lights go on, momentarily blinding me. I hear Pearl's laughter pealing around us.

When the white light that had exploded in my eyes clears, I see her. She is stretched out on the long kitchen table, nude, her finger- and toenails painted a dark shade of red, like dried blood.

"You boys hungry?" she smiles, demure as a geisha girl.

I grab one of her Chicago cutlery knives from the wooden block behind me and approach her.

"I'm going to slit your throat and drink your blood," I growl, "and then Lem here's going to turn you over and fuck your ass bloody with his nightstick."

"Oh, can't you please do that first while I'm still conscious?" she says in a small, pleading voice. "Please, please?"

"You'd like that, wouldn't you? No, don't speak," I reply as I press the knife to her throat. "How about I leave the blade right here and have Lem fuck you up the ass. But if you move even a bit you know the blade will cut into you. Hah? How about that?"

She moans.

"Then I could lick you up. You know how I like the taste of blood," I say. "You know I like the taste of blood, of come, of you."

I turn to Lem, who is standing watching us, his hand on his groin. "Get over here and take my jacket, boy. It's fucking hot in here."

I caress Pearl's body with the knife. She shivers as the blade travels over her skin.

"I told you we were coming to take you out," I say. "Isn't that what I said? But you're not dressed and ready to go, are you? What am I going to do with such a bad girl? I know Lem wants to shove his cock up your ass. But that's what you'd like, isn't it? Lem, let's tie her down and get serious. We'll go out later, Pearl girl," I pause to let my point sink in, "if you can still walk, that is."

Lem gets a length of rope and some restraints out of the bag. He stands Pearl on the floor and secures her feet to the table legs. Then he bends her over the table, chest down, and handcuffs her hands behind her back.

"There. Her ass is fixed but her head is free. Ready for all kinds of good things."

"I thought you got dressed up to take me out somewhere special," the girl pouts.

"But you're not dressed, are you? And where in hell did you hide all my socks? Hah? That reminds me. My bare feet are in these boots and it's none too comfortable."

She giggles.

"That's it. No more lip from you, Pearl girl. Lem,

stuff something in her mouth, would you?"

"Glad to."

He unzips his pants and kicks them off, the black straps of his jockstrap dark against the white cheeks of his buttocks.

Pearl sees what is coming and tries to get off the table.

"I don't want it," she whimpers.

I grip her shoulders tightly, the nails of my fingers digging into her skin.

"I'm not asking you what you want, Pearl girl, you're going to take what I give you, you hear?"

Lem settles himself on the table, his long legs stretched out in front of him. He pulls aside the jockstrap and his cock springs out of confinement.

"What a pretty cock, Pearl girl," I say, "let me see you kiss it good."

Lem unrolls a condom. He sits, legs spread wide, his cock stabbing the air. The grin on his face is as big as a slice of watermelon. I lower Pearl toward his crotch and she opens her mouth to take him in.

The sight of it makes me hard and wet and mad with desire all at once. I unbutton my leather pants, pull out my own cock, and repeat the ritual of the condom. Pearl's sucking is loud and greedy. Lem is grunting softly. I reach for Pearl's ass, grab the flesh to pull her to me, and enter her wet cunt in one quick motion. Pearl groans and expels the head of Lem's cock. I look up and see Lem's hand working at his crotch. The other hand is unbuttoning his blue cop shirt. He pulls Pearl's mouth to his big pink nipple.

I thrust into Pearl with all my might, breathing hard. After a while, Pearl begins to shout unintelligibly and I know she is about to come. Damn, so am I. No, I want to hold on longer. A little bit longer.

"Don't you come, Pearlie," I snarl, "not yet. Hold

on. Not yet."

"Uggghhh," she answers.

I pump her hard, as if my very life depended on it.

"Lem, you ready yet?"

"Yes, yes," he moans, "my hand is on my clit. Oh, yes, oh, yes, yes."

We all come together. And damn it's good.

firsts

"Dear Andrea:

"I've been gone from you for two days now. Have you caught up on your sleep yet? Hope so. It seems that neither of us gets more than three hours sleep when we're together. But don't get me wrong. It's not a complaint.

"When I got home the first thing I did was fetch the cats from Josey's. And were they ever mad at me! Then I slept for twelve hours straight.

"I have a lot of work to do so this will have to be a quickie. I know, I know. I told you I don't do quickies and I don't. I can't even kiss you just once.

"But this is a quickie. A quickie thank you note for a weekend of firsts. You know how I love my lists, so here it is:

      —birding
      —driving a motorcycle
      —handling your Beretta and going shooting
      —putting a condom on with my mouth
      —sucking your cock
      —getting fucked with a thigh harness
      —deflowering the boa dildo from Michigan
      —getting a cutting
      —begging

"You know, if anyone had told me a month ago that I would go birding I would have said: *Go where to do what?* But, yes, I enjoyed walking for miles, the weight of your binoculars in a harness across my chest. I loved seeing the birds. Common or not, they were all unfamiliar sightings to me. Red-tail hawk. Turkey vulture. Avocet. Goldfinch. Starling. Cedar waxwing. Great egret. Blue heron.

"It's the first time in over ten years that I've driven a motorcycle, and it was exhilarating to ride down country roads past endless fields of corn with the wind in my hair, the sun on my skin.

"You asked me about guns, said you had a Beretta. You handed it to me. I looked down the sightlines. You took me to a target range, taught me to load and shoot. I can still see you standing in front of me, feet apart, shoulders squared, the gun in your hands. I can smell the powder in the air, hear the sharp retort, feel the power. You were so proud of all my bull's-eyes.

"I know you find it hard to believe, but it is a first. I don't suck cock; girls suck my cock. And I loved getting fucked with your dildo anchored in the thigh harness. I liked your knee between my legs. I liked that your body was freer to climb all over me than if we had been joined hip to hip.

"Speaking of dildos, the boa dildo is beautiful. It was a glorious sight to see it entering you.

"Being cut with a scalpel was amazing. The feel of the blade as it cut into my flesh. The wails that came from my mouth.

"Oh, did I beg? All I said was...well, you remember. I don't think I want to write it down. Never. No way. What if someone else reads it? But we did discuss *never say never.* I always said I'd never suck cock or get a cutting.

"Until you.

"I had a great weekend. I can't remember the last time I've had so much fun. But, more importantly, I feel a bond between us, a connection top to top. Or, perhaps, it's heart to heart.

"Andrea, thank you for your laughter in my ears, your tongue in my mouth, your fist in my cunt, your gun in my hand, the blade in yours, your cock in my mouth, your hair in my face, my tears on your skin, my lips on your ass, my teeth on your back, my fingers in your wetness.

"In you.

"I'm forty-three and this is a first. When I hold you in my arms I don't want to let you go.

"Ever."

Firebrand Books is an award-winning feminist and lesbian publishing house committed to producing quality work in a wide variety of genres by ethnically and racially diverse authors.

You can buy Firebrand titles at your bookstore, or order them directly from the publisher (141 The Commons, Ithaca, New York 14850, 607-272-0000).

A free catalog is available on request.